Hello. This is Jane.

Judith Arcana's remarkable feat in *Hello. This is Jane.* is to paint, tile by tile, a complex mosaic of compelling linked stories—children's playgrounds and adult tattoo parlors, ill-advised lovers and underground abortion activists. In the mainstream and on the edges, you'll feel the urgency of the struggle for reproductive justice as you turn these pages.

    —Cindy Cooper, Founding Director of *Words of Choice*
and *The Reproductive Freedom Festival*

In a witty and searching voice, Arcana writes of resistance and revolutionary compassion, past, present, and future. Here is fiction rooted in the actual history of the Chicago underground abortion service known as JANE, which operated in the days before a woman's right to the procedure was legalized. Arcana herself was one of the young "Janes" providing abortions, and her tales of women helping women—the daring and secrecy, the risks and rewards—are essential reading, a warning and an inspiration for our time.

    —Kate Manning, Author of *My Notorious Life*, a novel

I'm profoundly grateful to Judith Arcana for writing these vital, electrifying stories. With abortion rights in America being stripped away—state by state, clinic by clinic—we need to hear from those who've fought this battle before. Arcana is a Jane; her work in the pre-Roe abortion underground has provided the seeds for her fiction, stories rooted in essential history to spark action in our terrifying present.

    —Leni Zumas, Author of *Red Clocks*

Hello. This is Jane.

STORIES BY
Judith Arcana

• LEFT FORK •

O'BRIEN, OREGON

ALSO BY JUDITH ARCANA

ANNOUNCEMENTS FROM THE PLANETARIUM
HERE FROM SOMEWHERE ELSE
SOON TO BE A MAJOR MOTION PICTURE
KEESHA AND JOANIE AND JANE
THE PARACHUTE JUMP EFFECT
4TH PERIOD ENGLISH
WHAT IF YOUR MOTHER
GRACE PALEY'S LIFE STORIES
EVERY MOTHER'S SON
OUR MOTHERS' DAUGHTERS

Author photo (p 214) by Michael Pildes, 1970

Back cover author photo courtesy NIRH

Cover image used with permission, courtesy of Don Deaton,
Sea Tramp Tattoo Company, Portland: Oregon's longest-running tattoo shop.
www.seatramptattoo.com

Layout and cover design by Ryan Forsythe

ISBN 978-1-945824-34-0
First Left Fork Edition: 3 May 2020

10 9 8 7 6 5 4 3 2 1

Left Fork
PO Box 110
O'Brien, OR 97534
www.leftfork.org

A Note to Readers

Some of the events in this book actually happened, and events *something like* some of the ones in this book happened too. Other events in this book are completely made up. The characters – their names, words, attitudes – have been invented.

*Fiction, nonfiction – they're made-up categories,
helpful for librarians and bookstores.
But it's all story. Really, it's all story.*

—Grace Paley

Hello. This is Jane.

Contents

Is there a sense in which a writer's vision gets more thoroughly and beautifully tested in a book of linked stories than it does in a collection of miscellaneous stories or a novel? How do linked-story collections combine the capaciousness of novels with the density and intensity of stories? Why do linked stories often have a stronger thematic pull than novels? How does each story in a collection of linked stories achieve closure-but-not-closure?

—David Shields

Answering the Question

Sandy's on a talk show, and she's talking; there's a YouTube clip that's getting a lot of play. In the clip, which opens with the camera focused on a tattoo on her right forearm (a small red apple with two little green leaves on its tiny stem), she's explaining how most people felt different forty-five years ago – different about contraception, abortion and motherhood in those years before the anti-abortion movement. Now she's getting to the part, about ten minutes in, where she says that sometimes people ask the Janes if anybody died.

Journalists, sociologists, undergraduates considering careers in what's now called healthcare delivery, people who show up in classrooms, auditoriums and bookstores where Janes are talking – they sometimes raise their hands in the q&a and ask if anybody died. Or they wait 'til the end, when the event is over and the Jane is being taken out for supper by the people who invited her to talk. Then they come up to her and ask, sometimes in almost a whisper, Did anybody die?

What they mean, Sandy thinks, is this: Did you kill anybody? The amazing thing about this question, she always says, is that the ones who ask it obviously expect the Jane to tell them. If that Jane thinks anyone in the Service killed somebody, the people who ask her think she'll tell them. So they start out with a belief in the honesty and integrity of the Janes. Isn't that kind of amazing?

The old phrase "butcher abortion" hardly ever turns up anymore, though "back-alley" is still popular for talking about the past and the rapidly-arriving future. That's the cultural history prompting such questions, Sandy thinks, because nobody who asks is hostile. Only the occasional anti, showing up to spit poison, is hostile – and they never ask this question because they already believe the Janes are *murderers*. In spite of their 21st century PR messaging, they think girls and women who have abortions are *baby-killers*. People who ask the question, though, really want to know what happened back then; some of them are so young they think the Service is the abortion Pleistocene of the USA. Of course, that's not the case – abortion history is way longer in North America, just like everywhere else, but they have no idea. Mostly, they just have no idea.

When she is the one asked, Sandy tells – like Denah, Lucy, Betsy and other Janes who are out – the only story they all know. Sandy's been speaking and organizing through the years anti-abortion people have been harassing women on clinic sidewalks, bombing buildings and shooting doctors, so when she's asked – like by that twenty-three year old Medical Student for Choice in Miami last January – she tells the only story she knows about somebody who died, a woman named Glenda Charleston. (Rachel used to say the woman's name was Selina – or that there was *another* woman who died the same way, and *that* woman's name was Selina.) They all know there were many women who died because abortion was illegal and inaccessible – women who'd never heard of the Janes, or heard too late. *So* many women. But there was only this one they knew about for sure, so *her* terrible story was the terrible story they told.

Sandy says, talking to the host behind the long desk, looking into the camera: Some Janes say the woman's name was Selina, but I was told her name was Glenda. One time I heard somebody say she'd actually used a coat hanger; another time it was a knitting needle. Truth is though, nobody in the Service knew what she'd done before she called us; she didn't tell us anything. She just showed up for her appointment like everybody else.

She hadn't told her counselor she already tried to do it – and she'd probably lied about how far along she was, too. There were always women and girls who lied or said they didn't know, because they were afraid. They thought we wouldn't do it if they said the wrong date – you know, the wrong number of weeks – *too many weeks.*

She, Glenda or Selina, even faked her temperature. They'd left her alone with the thermometer in her mouth, and she must've taken it out or shaken it down, so her infection fever didn't register.

She was desperate, and desperation made her body so rigid they couldn't get the speculum in; they had to massage her thighs and perineum for almost fifteen minutes. When she finally relaxed, a rush of thick yellow pus came out. The pus poured out of her vagina, down the speculum, all over her thighs, all down the plastic sheet. Then they knew. Even the sweat smell, before that, had seemed normal. I mean, they thought it was only *fear*, you know? Janes were used to that.

She was shaking while they cleaned her, sobbing and talking in that kind of whisper-shout you do sometimes with panic. They were telling her she had to go to the hospital, telling her Arlene would leave right then and take her, drive her right from there to the emergency room. But she just kept saying No. No. No. No. Her voice rasped when she said she couldn't, could *not*, have that baby. She could hardly breathe. Her eyes and her crying were wild. She screamed, I brought money!

Arlene and MaryAnn talked about it that night, telling Sandy *they* were practically shaking when they took out the speculum and carefully, gently, washed her; how Glenda was trying to get up while they worked; how she pulled her clothes on and rushed out of the apartment; how they tried to but could not stop her when she ran down the stairs. They had the phone number she'd given, but nobody answered when they called. They called for two days and nights, and nobody answered.

Then, on the third night, somebody picked up the phone. He said, Miss Glenda's passed. I'm so sorry to have to tell you like this. She's gone. This is her pastor speaking. Would you like to talk to a member of the family?

Betsy Is Interviewed For
Tattoo Queen's Website
Biography Series

Some things you just realize you know, like how to behave on the subway. Other things you have to study and practice, like a new language, or how to stand on your head. I decided to learn about tattoos. How I did it was I spent a certain amount of time around what used to be called *parlors*, watching the work being done, studying the flash on the walls and in the books. In Chicago I mostly liked the place on Broadway in Uptown, where I got work done by an old guy named Jerry. Jerry was quirky; you might even say he was *difficult* – and he was really good.

Now, this was Chicago in the early 1970's. I hung around the local artists and read about the famous ones, their style and attitude and how different they could be – some guys wanting it to be art, some laughing at that even when it was. I heard them talk about single needles, slender like wires, and bunches soldered into three, five, seven or nine-liners. They knew the speed of the gun by sound; they could tell if it was racing or dragging. They'd say, Let's go seven-wide on this one, and make thick curves, blending their fast little circles, mixing their own color when the basics couldn't take them where they wanted to go. Pretty quick I learned that work done over bone and tendon hurt more than work over muscle and fat, and I felt the sting of the thinnest needle on the inside flesh of my elbow. Once I took my vacation in San Francisco so I could visit Lyle Tuttle's museum and studio. I read tattoo magazines and taped their pages up on my walls. I read books about Japan and New Guinea, articles about sailors. I read about people all over the world who used tattoo for thousands of years – that's how I learned tattooing is magic.

People always ask the same questions, even now that all the kids are tattooed so it's everywhere, more than forty years after I started. I answer truthfully: Yes, it hurts; but you know, it's over so quickly and then you have this picture in your skin, part of you for the rest of your life. How many things that hurt you leave you marked with magic? Not too many, right? Because the question, Did it hurt? always makes me think, Compared to what? Whiplash? Paper cuts? Childbirth? What are we talking about here? What do they mean, what are they actually thinking when they ask about pain? There was one woman I met at a party – she had a purple orchid by Cliff Raven on her breast – who whisper-talked about how *pain* was one of the things that really *excited* her about tattooing, but she was strange; no one else ever said that to me. People who are into pain can always find something that'll last longer and go deeper than the quick silver needles of tattoo.

So yes, it hurts. But no, I'm not afraid of getting a disease. These days that's a hot one, lots more people wonder about that now; they're thinking HIV, hepatitis – the big stuff. But I say, No, I'm not afraid, because I'm thoughtful, you know? I choose these people the way you choose anybody you pay to touch your body: carefully. How did you choose your doctor, your hair cutter? How about people who give you a massage? They never thought about it that way. Some of them are afraid of needles; turns out that's pretty common. They don't get vaccinations or acupuncture either.

Talking to needlephobes, I got a surprise from my own memory. Here's the thing: I was tattooed as a child. When I was in kindergarten, there was a plan to mark all US citizens with our blood type. Maybe it was a Cold War thing, like those bomb drills where we rushed out into the halls and crouched against the lockers. I don't know. They hung sheets on dividers across the stage in the auditorium and lined up everybody, from us little ones through twelfth grade, in the aisles. When you got to the stage, you climbed the stairs and went into a little sheet-walled cubicle where a man in a white coat lifted up your striped tee-shirt and shot A, B, AB or O positive or negative into your ribs with what he called "the needle gun." They told us, like they always do, that it wouldn't hurt, and they gave us notes to take home to our parents explaining the marks on our skin. Those were the days when schools would pretty much do what they wanted, and parents were pretty much grateful for whatever that was. But the little letters they shot at me didn't last. That first tattoo disappeared; I have no trace left of my O+, and will never know if it could have saved my life when the Russians sailed into the Great Lakes to invade Gary, Indiana.

Anyway – no wonder I was never surprised that small children were the best tattoo observers. They're completely honest, and there's a lot they want to know: What is that? Where'd you get it? Could you have any picture you want? Can you change it? Can you get more? Could I get one? Could you give me one? I know their parents want me to say things like, It's not for children. It really hurts a lot. You have to wait until you grow up. But I don't. I'm always straight with them and after I tell them about the needles, I tell them to use fake tattoos to try out designs until they find something they want to have forever. Children love to think about forever.

There was a time when people would ask me if it was permanent. Then, maybe in the early nineties, they started to ask if it was real; but hardly anybody asks those questions now, because having a tattoo now is about as distinctive as having freckles. Like, some people have 'em, some people don't, it's no big deal, nothing to talk about. And this is too bad, because I realized somewhere along the years that I liked being stared at in the summer when most of mine were showing. And I liked being a surprise in the winter; people couldn't hold onto their assumptions when I rolled up my sleeves. The manager and vitamin buyer of the biggest upscale health food store in the Great Lakes region was *not* a skank – and they already knew that, so they had to adjust their minds when they saw my tattoos. They were used to asking my advice and hearing me say things like: It's best to use a supplement that includes bioflavonids along with vitamin C. Or: Large daily quantities of vitamin C may cause frequent urination. They didn't associate the use of phrases like "may cause frequent urination" with images they might have of tattooed women, so they had to adjust their minds. I liked that.

Some people couldn't adjust, of course. Some people didn't want to. I remember exactly what my Aunt Leona said to me – when I showed her my first one, done by Jerry when I turned 21. She said, But Betsy – why would you want to do that to yourself? She sounded repulsed, maybe offended, so I didn't even try to explain. I could tell she was one of those people. But I always thought up things to say to the people who were not repulsed, the ones who were drawn to me out on the street, attracted by my illustrations, excited by what I'd done.

Why did I do it? First of all, I found out I could have beauty. I looked in the mirror in 1970, and saw that I was news. By the time of my 21st birthday I was getting used to it. Like I would be at the lake, and my hair would be blowing across my face and the sun would be shining through so it had more colors than only brown, or I would look down at the shape of my thighs in my jeans, or I would lay back and watch somebody's hands move up my belly on their way to my breasts. I figured that even if I got only twenty-one more years, starting right then I had my whole life to live over. I wanted to celebrate. I wanted to decorate myself. That tattoo was a sign that said I knew who I was, and if you read my sign you would know too. Most of the signs from before that time said CAUTION or YIELD or STOP, but I was done with those.

Some things you do on purpose because they're smart, some you do because they'll make you laugh. Other things make you feel strong, or sexy; they remind you of your best dreams. Some you do for beauty as much as anything else, and that's got to be the case with tattoo. When I started out, women getting done was unusual, especially if you weren't a biker chick or a hooker. Women with visible tattoos had power of a kind I'd never imagined. Guys on the street were surprised; they were turned on, they dug it; it made them stop *pushing* the way they usually do. You know how they are, like if their kissy lips don't make you spread your legs right there on the sidewalk, then you're an ugly bitch? But with tattoos, those men changed. They acted like they thought I could bust them; they were willing to watch me go by without paying their toll. And without the toll, I wanted them to watch. I wanted everybody to watch.

Another thing, that I didn't think then but think now, is this: tattooing is all about bodies. *It's something you do with your body.* And in those days, those years, we – women – were all about our bodies. You know that book, *Our Bodies, Ourselves*? That title didn't come out of anybody's imagination; it came out of endless conversation. We were talking and thinking about ourselves, our female selves, *as bodies* – what we knew, or didn't, about what they are, how they work, what they look like, what we're allowed to do with them. What we're allowed to do with them was a big part of it (and what we let other people do with our bodies, or what they did with our bodies even when we didn't want them to). The body/ mind thing then, before everybody got all Zen about it, was basically this: we used our minds to figure out our bodies, and our bodies made lots of work for our minds.

There are rules for what you can do with your body if you're a woman, and forty years ago, tattooing wasn't on the list – not hardly. Getting tattooed was major transgression against the body rules for women. The few women who were tattooed were discounted, dismissed, disapproved – seriously dissed. (Unless they were stars. Rock stars. Movie stars. For stars, tattooing was like anything else in their sparkly lives – something allowed, or even encouraged, by fame.)

Like a lot of other women who grew up and woke up after the middle of the twentieth century, I was into transgression, bigtime. I understand that now. Like with other body stuff women began to do then – and do like crazy now. Sports – for sure – and piercing. Even abortion (not like women haven't been doing that *forever*). Abortion's kind of related to tattooing if you think about it, because in this country, in what they call *the social contract*, abortion's all about biology and law. Somebody should study that, you know? Those two, together?

Once I answered an ad in the free weekly to model for a photography show up on North Halsted, and got a full set of prints as payment for the session. This woman showed up with boxes of gear and had me change clothes a lot so she could get shots with different ones showing. On the walls of the gallery, the card by each picture listed artists' names for all the tattoos. Jerry, who had done a couple more for me, liked the publicity so much he offered to do my next one free. But when I came in for it we had a fight, because he said he wouldn't do a blossom without a stem, a rose with no leaves or thorns. And that was what I wanted: the blossom of a partly-open black rose, heart like a cervix. He pointed out that this was his opinion and he was entitled to it. I've never disagreed with that particular position, and since he was nowhere near the only game in town, I dropped the subject. Jerry had already given my right shoulder some Japanese waves cresting over rocks, put a sleeping tiger on

my left hip and wound a daisy chain around my right wrist.
But after the fight, like people say, we agreed to disagree.

I never got a butterfly on my ass, a rosebud on my breast, a
little red heart on my thigh. That's what the few women who
did walk into tattoo parlors in those days were expected to
get. Janis Joplin, with her sweet Raggedy Ann "I love you"
riding up against her raggedy voice, probably influenced
some of us, but I can't remember another star getting a
tattoo that mattered. Anyway, the bear, the goldfish and the
black rose were all done by Zack, who had no opinions.
His chair was the last one, way in back; you couldn't see
him from the street. Written on his mirror were words
from a song by The Band: "…ain't no pretender/wanna see
my tattoo?" One day I was hanging around and Zack said,
You still want that black rose, no stem, thorns or leaves? Sit
down and show me where you want it. He was a quiet guy
with a good memory. He looked at what you brought in to
show him, listened to what you said. Then he'd say, I can
do that. Sometimes while he was working on you, he'd say,
This part's gonna hurt. Or with a really big job, he might
say, Let's take a little breather here.

When some of my girlfriends said they wanted to get
tattoos, I sent them to Jerry and Zack; between the two of
them, we could get whatever we wanted. It was like finding
a great place to get your hair cut. Sally, who was six feet tall
and wanted a big fat red rose on her bicep, couldn't get it
from Jerry, who thought her red rose should be small, and
not on her bicep. So she got what she wanted from Zack,
though Jerry put a pair of blue carnations on her ankle.
Rachel, a tiny woman with thick black wavy hair that made
a cape across her neck, got a viper twisted around her upper
arm – from Zack. Jerry put the pair of ruby hummingbirds
on Janine's shoulder blades, and they are still remarkable,
even now they've faded some. Janine's tattoos were the
first ones I ever saw on a woman in a movie – she was in

a documentary about women's bodies made by some film student at the art museum. She looked terrific. You might want to get her for this interview series!

They had classic flash and some talented guys in 1970, no question. You could see that as soon as you came in the door. There was a whole section on the solar system, not just the suns and moons you see everywhere. Everybody had the sun fierce or smiling, the moon and stars in a set or singles. But at Jerry's you could get the Milky Way spread across your back. I knew about one other good place, near Wrigley Field by the el, but I never needed to go there.

I loved to hang around Jerry's place, to watch them doing it, to listen to people who came in telling what they wanted, to see the designs come out of the books and onto the skin. They had a small section of exotic cars, but they also had a jeep and a VW bus – those were the only ones with no flames coming out their exhaust pipes. There were license plates with state slogans; New Hampshire's *Live Free or Die* was probably the most popular, mounted next to the shields and eagles, the quivers of arrows and all the guns. They had rocket launchers, bazookas, rifles, steely blue-black and shiny silver pistols, and a cannon good enough for any state courthouse lawn.

Like all the parlors, they had animals, including some mean looking rats and a few cute mice, but the really fabulous ones were the snakes, fanged and coiled. Coral snakes would slither around your wrist or neck or they could slide around your whole body, ankle to chin. There were horses on a separate panel, wild mustangs I always thought must be spooked by the snakes, thoroughbreds with or without jockeys in silks, and of course, straight out of the sixties, there were blue and white unicorns any size you wanted – some lying down by their virgins, who always had hair like Joni Mitchell.

Once I drove out to a tent circus in Pecatonica to meet the tattooed woman. She had all the presidents of the United States – Garfield and Cleveland made faces when she bent her elbows, FDR and his cousin Teddy's chins curved over her shoulders. She was born to it. Her father and brothers were acrobats, she told me, pointing to a trapeze artist flying over one thigh and a pyramid of men in tights stretching around the other. Across her belly, her own mother did a single-hand stand on the bare back of a horse that looked like Trigger in the movies. I'd read about her in the paper, and went out there looking, maybe, for wisdom, for words about the life of the body from a woman older than I was then. She had a full blown red rose on each breast, the tips of her nipples centering their petals; a slim bright snake circled her neck, its head and forked tongue darting down her collar bone. The stems of the roses and the snake's long body slipped between the presidents' heads so dark green leaves and bright yellow diamonds showed up in sharp contrast to the complexions of a new Lyndon Johnson and an old James Madison. She had no empty space but her face; even her hands and feet were done, her fingers and toes in colored stripes like the rainbow that curved around her right hip, slipping back into the crease between the cheeks of her ass, suggesting a tiny pot of gold inside. She was amused by me with my half dozen pictures, but she was kind, sharing her tuna sandwich and telling me stories about her lover, a juggler. The lover was also tattooed, and traveled with the circus in season, but wouldn't show herself to anybody who didn't have work of their own; she didn't feel good about that.

Well, it's a youth thing now – and it's high art; nearly every punk in the back of the Broadway bus has good work: designs from New Guinea, totems from the Pacific Northwest nations, Celtic symbols. And these are kids who are going to college, kids with money. There was a little while in the early nineties when the young ones first took it up, there'd be kids who would stop to talk, to ask about the work and show their own stuff, just like anybody who comes up and says, Nice tattoo – and shows me theirs. But this hardly ever happens anymore with the young ones. I guess most kids don't think it's cool to talk to a woman my age about anything, maybe especially about something they think is theirs. You know how when you're young you need to own anything that matters to you? With kids, it's got to be their thing, and it can't be your thing – and if it is your thing they don't want it to be their thing anymore. You know what I mean?

But the ones who do their own, in the joint or in the alley, scratching with pins they clean in the flame of a match, are still what they always were: outlaws, and their markers look as rough as ever. I met a few in my day. We say that when we get over fifty – *in my day* – as if our days were not the same as anybody's, or at least overlapping. I did see some people who rolled their own. Marco, the guy who used to sweep up at the barber shop next door to where I worked, had designs all up and down his arms, mostly cars and eagles. He'd done the ones on his left arm, he said, but the right arm was done by his uncle, who taught him how to do it. He learned how in high school, Marco said. You can bet that's mostly all what my uncle learned in high school. He said he had some on his legs too, but he didn't offer to show them, and that was ok with me. Once I met a fifteen year old girl in the women's lockup at Eleventh and State. (Don't even ask what *I* was doing there.) She was five months pregnant and had scratched the name she chose for the baby into her arm: Buddy.

Marco and Buddy's mama seemed to want the same thing I did from the pictures in our skin. That was a while ago now, when a lot of us were affectionate about our tattoos, proprietary but willing to share in our special kind of show-

and-tell. Me, I always hated to see a new tattoo disappear under the bandage. Just done, they were so bright, the skin all wet and slightly swollen like sex – but I did get off on the waiting time, when you'd be walking around with the design all wrapped up, and everybody would say, What happened? I'd uncover mine about twenty times a day, to rub whatever the guy told me onto the scab, making the tattoo shine again for a minute.

Once I went to a party with a strip of disposable diaper wrapped around my wrist – that was the bandage of choice at the time, like the plastic wrap they use in some shops now. That night I wore my Frye boots, a red knit halter top and a long skirt, the kind we made out of old jeans. We would cut open the legs and stitch fabric into the openings, front and back; mine had velvet patches in front and old silk neckties in back. I was looking pretty good, but the eye catcher at that party was definitely my wrist. People came up to me, pointed at my wrist, touched it, even lifted it – gently, so sweetly they reached for that wrist, as if it were a baby, there in its diaper. They crooned, Aw, what's the matter? Are you hurt? And when I told them it was a new tattoo, a daisy chain, just done that day, they stroked the skin around the bandage, stroked my hand, said ooh and ahh and oh. They wanted to know when it would be done, healed, ready. When they could see it. Would I call them when I took off the bandage, could they watch when I took off the bandage, could they come over and help me take off the bandage? That tattoo got more action all covered up than the ones that were already out on my arms and shoulders.

I still visit tattoo shops when I travel, but I think my skin is maybe too slack for new work. I'm past sixty after all, so I'll probably stick with what I've got. If I do decide to go for more, I'd like to find an artist around my age, maybe a woman who's seen all this go by, like me. I never got tattooed by a woman; I was too early. Maybe I'd pick out a classic, right off the flash on the wall. Maybe I'd get a ribbon; I've never done that, never had a word put on my body. What word would it be? Not my own name; I carry ID for that. What if I pick a name no one I know even has – and then be mysterious about it when people ask: *Pansy, Maritza* or *Franklin*. Maybe a slogan, like the boys: *Born to Raise Organic Vegetables*. Or I could just pick something I like the sound of: *crunchy, illumination, quack*. Maybe a comment, like *Very Funny*. Let people make what they want out of that.

Hello. This is Jane.

1. *Jane at Work*

The May morning is already bright but Denah and Eli are deep in sleep; it's maybe six when the phone rings, startling them awake. The phone's on his side of the bed.

Hullo? Huh? Yeah, just a minute. He hands the phone to Denah, rocking her shoulder and mouthing silently, It's for *Jane*.

Denah sits up to get clear. Hello? Yes, this is Jane. Who's this?

Her voice gets stronger. What's happening? Where are you?

Denah sits all the way up, against the headboard. Ok. Now, wait, please stop talking for a second and take a few deep, slow breaths. She breathes into the phone, a model. Then, suddenly, she throws herself across the bed, across Eli, and slams the phone down.

Omygod, Eli! Get up – there's a woman, across the street at Grant, she's there right now, she went there to miscarry. Some doctor has been threatening her, and she's hysterical – he grabbed the phone right out of her hand just now – yelled at me – says he knows where I am! He said, *We know who you are. We know where you are.* He says they're coming right now!

Eli sits up fast and says, Let's look. They jump off the bed, rush to the front window, the side of their building that faces the hospital. The street is empty, silent.

Denah is wild-eyed; Eli is calm. He puts his hands on her shoulders and says, Let's get out of here.

Yes! And we have to get the Jane stuff out! Jesus! Eli – I have everything! The cards, the file, the phone machine, the beeper – it's all here.

We'll take care of it. He's getting dressed as he talks. We're going to put everything – all of it – in my golf bag. I'll go out like always, down the fire escape. You go out the door, walk toward the lake on Webster. I'll meet you in the car at the corner of Clark. In the car we'll figure out where to go.

They're both dressed now – cut-offs, t-shirts, glasses; she pushes the Jane gear into his bag, he slides in a couple pairs of socks and stuffs a jacket on top. They're out of the apartment in less than four minutes, at the corner of Clark Street in less than two more.

Eli drives south on small streets, zig-zagging like a Jane on a work day. They stop at a gas station past Roosevelt Road, so Denah can call Allie.

Allie opens the door of her Hyde Park apartment wearing a bathrobe and long sparkly earrings. Her face is puffy from sleep. When they're inside, she goes to her front window and looks out.

Nothing. I think it was a bluff. He didn't really know where you were, or who you are. You weren't her counselor – she just called you Jane. Why did she even have your number?

I said Rita could give it to her for backup, in case Rita couldn't deal with whatever she needed when labor started. You know, the kids or something. So she gave her my number and just told her it was another Jane. But here's the thing – if they have that number, they can get the name&address from Reverse Information – I don't know why they didn't, or haven't. Or maybe they did. Maybe they have – by now.

Eli says, Well, maybe she didn't have it written down. Maybe she memorized it.

Denah and Allie look at him.

Allie says to Denah, More likely she dialed before he came in, so the number wasn't sitting out there when he busted in on her and grabbed the phone. If he had that number, maybe he *would* have done what he said; they'd've been in your apartment before you were out of it. I think he doesn't have it. He doesn't know. He can't know. Who he is and how he thinks, every day of his life, keep him from knowing who we are and what we do. Guys like that never know these things because they can't – lucky for us – imagine them.

Eli dodged around on the way here – we didn't take the Drive. I'm sure nobody followed us. But I want to leave everything here for a while, Allie. At the next meeting we can decide – if nothing's happened – where it all should be, whether it's safe to keep it at my place again.

In the car on the way home Eli says, It's not safe to have that stuff at our place, Denah. It never was, and now for sure. How much closer do they have to be – I mean, that hospital is across the street, forgodsake.

If nothing happens, I think Allie is right – he was bluffing. There's no reason to change anything.

There is silence in the car. Then Eli says, How about this for a reason? The end of June'll be five months, you'll be starting to look pregnant, easy to spot; maybe it'll be harder for you

Judith Arcana

to move fast. And there's me, too, Denah. My place in all this, what I think, my feelings – my law license! That's not a reason?

Let's see what happens. We don't have to decide anything right this minute.

They are quiet again, driving along the lake. It's maybe seven now, and the light on the water is turning to gold.

Then Eli says, Ok. Ok. So – was she wearing those earrings while she was sleeping? Those long earrings, at six-thirty in the morning? I mean, did she wear them to bed? Or did she put them on when you called, because we were coming over? Or what? What *about* that? I mean, you gotta wonder.

* * *

Later the same day, Lucy is standing at the checkout counter in a medical supply house. She's got six dozen clear plastic vaginal specula in various sizes, packed in plastic bags. When her turn at the register comes, she pays cash. When the clerk asks the name of her company for the receipt, she says, North Side Women's Clinic.

She heads home, stopping at the drug store on the way, leaving all the bags on the floor in the back of the car, her jacket tossed over them. Pushing hard on the revolving door – it's got one of those wind-stopping rubber panels attached at the bottom – she flashes on yesterday afternoon, when she stopped at that day's apartment to ask the working Janes what supplies they'd need.

She knew Betsy was working; she thought maybe they'd have lunch together and she'd return Betsy's copy of *Zelda*. As Lucy walked down the hall, she heard a gasp from one of the bedrooms and looked in. The woman on the bed had blood pumping out of her vagina, hard. It hit the wall behind Jake before he could cover the open speculum with one hand and reach with the other for Kleenex, Kotex, a towel – whisper-shouting to Betsy, Ice trays! Fast!

Today, now, at the drug store, the cash register clerk says, Gosh, you buy so much alcohol every week! If this was Prohibition I'd think you were making bathtub gin! He smiles at her.

Lucy is startled out of her memory of the day before by his apt comparison, but makes herself smile back and laugh a little. She says, I make jewelry, and I clean the beads, the wires, and the backing of semi-precious stones with alcohol.

When she tells this story at home to Mary Jo – who, as usual these days, is not amused – she laughs and says, And while I'm saying this, I'm hoping the guy doesn't know any more about making jewelry than I do, which is pretty much nothing. She hasn't told Mary Jo about the day before, about Jake and the woman with the blood and the ice, even though everything turned out ok. The woman is fine, but that's not the part Mary Jo would focus on.

Lucy and Mary Jo live rent-free in the Service's northside midwife apartment, where women come to miscarry when they are too far along in their pregnancies for the Service to do a D&C.

Mary Jo says, I don't see how you can think that's funny. I don't see why you don't think that's dangerous – and scary. You'll make a joke out of anything, even *this*.

Look, Mary Jo, this is how you can live here without paying rent; how else would we get to live in a place like this? In a neighborhood turning rundown crap into middle class heaven all around us? Besides, you knew what the deal was when you moved in.

I didn't know what it would be like! I couldn't imagine it in advance!

You're an artist, for chrissake! You've got a rich imagination – a psychedelic imagination, in fact. You're the first woman I ever met who had a tattoo – not counting Janis Joplin but ok, I haven't really *met* her. That suggests creativity, even open-mindedness. Doesn't it?

I mean it about this not being funny, Lucy. But look, it doesn't matter what the reason is. Fact is, I can't stand it. I probably shouldn't stay here. I probably shouldn't have moved here in the first place. And, I gotta say, I have trouble thinking *you* should. Shit, Lucy, I have trouble thinking you *do* this!

Ok, fine. We've been heading this way for a while, I know. This conversation is even a little overdue. If you can't stay, you can't stay. But I want you to tell me the truth – is this about being Catholic? Is this because you think it's a sin? Do you think I'm bad, wrong? That all these women are bad and wrong?

I never go to church, certainly not to confession; I never pray – you know that.

Yeah, well, I eat bacon, lettuce and tomato sandwiches, but that doesn't mean my rotten relationship with my sister won't cross my mind on Yom Kippur. Just tell me. I need to know. Is it religion? Or is it just that these terrified women show up at our place in the middle of the night with contractions – and the cops could bust in here any time? *That* I can understand. Because that's what I think – often.

Well, *I* think that over at St Bartholomew's, even Father Sweeney, that shithead with his threats of hellfire, couldn't possibly compete with *this* stuff! It's all of what you said, Lucy; it's *all* of that – and the fact you're so exhausted most of the time. Even when you're *not* on call, when we both have a break and could fool around, go to a movie, get high. I want you to be healthy, I want us to be happy – we're young! Jesus, Lucy, we're still kids! You shouldn't have all this responsibility!

There's a pause at this possibly offensive and probably ridiculous statement, a pause in which Lucy eyes her, waiting.

Mary Jo continues. Ok, yeah, I suppose sometimes I do think about what the nuns taught me. How could I not? They were so heavy, with their full-out habits, so intense, they left a big impression on me. To say the least. And even though I didn't like them, what they said came in – it came in, and it's still part of me.

What if we got Father Sweeney to join those guys in Concerned Chicago Clergy or whatever they call it – the ones who do abortion counseling. Think that'd help?

Everything's a joke to you – or, if it isn't to start with, you make it that way. Some things just aren't funny, Lu.

* * *

That night on the phone, Lucy says to Denah, I guess *both* Eli and Mary Jo are quitting the Jane Auxiliary . . . Right, right, I know he didn't say it as clearly as she did, but isn't that because he avoids making statements like that whenever he can? Good as he is – and he sure was great with that golf bag thing – isn't it more his way to do it in his mind, unconsciously maybe, and then later his behavior shows where he's gone with it? Haven't we talked about this before? Isn't that what happened the time you had the big fight with throwing things? The grapefruit and tomato scene?

Oh, Lucy, maybe they'll leave *together* and scandalize everybody, the whole spectrum. We'd be the sympathetic victims of a sex puzzle. That'd make my life simpler. How many times will I have to decide about this marriage? Is this the karma thing, where you're faced with the same circumstances over and over until you learn your lesson? No – isn't that supposed to be in different lifetimes? Not all in one, like this? ... You think I'm kidding? I only *sound* like I'm kidding. Actually, I'm too serious to sound like what I really mean... Oh, I'm sorry to mix my schtick with your scene, honey. I know you want Mary Jo to stay – your situation is different.

Yeah, but why? ... I mean, why do I want her to stay if she doesn't want to be here? Why do I want a girlfriend who disapproves of my work, my ideas, my politics? ... Yeah, I do want *a girlfriend*. I wouldn't be happy alone. I always get a kick out of the bar scene, but I hate the idea of *looking* – you know? I just wish she'd admit this is part of real life – part of the real world... I don't expect her to be like a Jane, you know, think like a Jane, talk like a Jane, make jokes like a Jane – I don't need that stuff from Mary Jo. What I want is for her to understand we're like everybody else. Undertakers tell death jokes; surgeons talk on the golf course about what they find when they cut you open; teachers gossip about students. It's normal!

But Lucy, not even all the Janes think this way, so what do you want from Mary Jo? You think Mandy talks the way we do, you and me? You think Lola does? And she's got the disadvantage of her upbringing... Please, I know that. When Catholic women get going, they can be stupendous – those radical nuns! But that's not who Mary Jo is. She was honest with you, you gotta give her that... Well, you gotta give her *something*.

2. *Jane's Day Off*

Sandy, MaryAnn and Rachel are sprawled in the grass near the Lincoln Park lagoon, close to the zoo. Sandy is inhaling, talking while sucking in smoke. She says, This is good weed.

Handing on the joint, MaryAnn says, My cousin brought it last weekend, gave me a nice fat little baggie. I couldn't use it the whole week because I was working so much. Oh, hey, did Lucy tell you her idea about creating a new doll – called "Janie"? She thought up a whole set of pregnancy action figures with lotsa *stuff*, the way Barbie and her team have *stuff*. So there's Abortion Janie, Pregnant Janie, and New Mommy Janie. There's a tiny speculum, curettes, syringes, teensy antibiotic pills, teensy sanitary napkins, and lots of gear for the New Mommy doll to take care of her teensy baby doll. Lucy is hilarious.

Rachel says, Do you notice we seem to be working a lot more now? Is that my imagination? I have this fantasy that somewhere there are commercials advertising the Service, on tv or radio or something, bringing in more women.

It's because Allie and Paula are both NOT working – Allie's in California and Paula's sick. I think there's not enough Janes; we need another orientation session, to get some more workers. Do you think our fearless leaders will notice this, or should we suggest it? Sandy laughs out her sarcasm.

You can suggest it, Sandy – they never pay attention to what I say. But, yeah, the numbers just keep going up. I thought since it got to be legal in New York, we'd have *less* work, but that's not what's happening. There's *more*. Is that crazy?

No, think about it – New York going legal gave it more prominence, but only women with money can go to New York. Women who have to sell their stereos, sell their clothes, those women come to the Service. And I guess by now everybody here knows about us. So the volume is increasing. There must be some relevant principle of economics applicable here.

Principle of economics?!

Yeah! Come on! You know this! I mean, who are we talking about? Rich women have always been able to get abortions – and they always will. They pay their own doctors thousands of dollars and call it "therapeutic." You can bet it *is* therapeutic. Or they fly to Puerto Rico. Japan. England. I mean, do rich women come through the Service? Our women never have chunks of money available fast; they've got no margin – since access to knowledge and access to money are, guess what, related, they have no resources, no information, they don't know what's possible and they couldn't pay for it if they did.

What are you, Milton Friedman crossed with Betty Friedan? No, I'm kidding you. That was a good riff. Use it for the graduate school application.

Hey, did you see what Gert did to Mandy at the meeting Tuesday? That could be the most vicious cut yet. I can't believe Mandy puts up with it, lets herself be talked to that way!

What's really bizarre about it is, Mandy's a good worker. She's thorough, she's skilled, she's kind to the women, she puts them at ease. I'm not saying I want to go dancing with Mandy, she's definitely not my type, but I mean, come on – what's the fucking problem?

Oh, her work isn't the problem – it's irrelevant – that's not what's happening at all. Look, if we're talking about the Service, I mean, *the work*, then, yeah, sure, Mandy's just fine. But if we're talking about the Service in terms of the people in it, the group dynamics, people's relationships, then we're talking about something else, right?

Hello. This is Jane.

Yeah, then we're talking about some people who – a very small number of people who – don't know how to behave. Didn't anybody ever tell them to make nice? We need little blinking signs, or messages tattooed on our foreheads: BE NICE.

Rachel says, Sometimes I'm shocked when Gert's mean to Mandy, because she's always sweet to me. I like her. And listen, Gert takes on so much responsibility in the Service.

That's one way of seeing her power, sure. But it's like when my grandma launches into her cliché-ridden routine about how even though Mussolini was a fascist who paired up with Hitler, he was good for Italy because he got the country to shape up – the trains running on time and all that blah blah blah.

Lola told me Gert's got trouble with her husband, even that he flirts with other Janes – is that true? Have you heard that? That could make her pretty unhappy, you know.

But is it Mandy he supposedly flirts with?

Who knows? What's really amazing, and's been true the whole year I've been a Jane, is this: that shit does not come out in a work day; it never happens in front of the women.

True, yeah, amazing in fact, but can that last? I'm always *afraid* it's gonna happen, like if Gert is assisting when Mandy is, or they're working the front together?

No, no, no. That pairing won't come up. Everybody knows the deal. Everybody doing the scheduling knows – nobody would ever put them together. Look, do you think this isn't what goes on everywhere, all the time, where people work? Clinics, hospitals, schools, stores, offices, supermarkets?

I can't believe it'll never happen – what about emergencies? What about sudden schedule changes? I can't believe –

MaryAnn interrupts: Hey! Hey! I'll tell you what *I* can't believe: I can't believe *you two*! I can't believe I brought you this amazing dope on a day off and you are wasting it – talking about work! Talking about Gert, for chrissake! That manipulative bitch. Could we leave the world of unhappy women and their fetuses for a little while? It's late April and almost warm as June! Come on – look at that gull, the one floating above the edge of the lagoon – it's had its wings spread out like that for an hour, I swear, like it's trying out for the role of Classic Gull. Floating on the air. Like an urban hawk. Like a bird-angel.

Sandy leans back, looks up, says, Yeah. It's quintessential gull.

Rachel falls slowly backward onto the grass and says, Yeah. Iconic gull, gull *qua* gull – ah, ok. Uh huh. Ok.

* * *

Right about the time Sandy and Rachel succumb to the sky, the gull and the weed, Denah and Claudia are in Claudia's kitchen with three children. Denah's baby, Joey, is crawling on the floor, eating bits he picks up, grazing like a small chubby goat. The women are packing up to go to the park.

Denah says, Uh-oh, I smell something new in the air of the warm spring kitchen. Claudia, would you finish these sandwiches while I change Joey? They all have peanut butter, but only one has jelly so far.

Chloe responds instantly, jumping up from the table where she's been fitting measuring cups and spoons together by size, calling out: *I* want to put jelly on. *I* want to put jelly on.

Sam, who's sitting beside Chloe reading the funnies, says, *I* don't.

Claudia helps Chloe onto a tall stool beside the counter, takes the end piece of a loaf of bread, swipes a butter knife through the jelly and hands it to her daughter, saying, You put jelly on this one. Then she turns to the slices already covered with peanut butter and slathers them rapidly with jelly.

Sam says, Is there something else? I want something else. His mother says, Yes! There are two something elses: carrot chunks and apple slices. We know who we're with.

Ok, Mom. I just had to check. I had to be sure.

Denah's voice comes in from the hall, as she changes the baby's diaper: Claud, let's be sure to stop at the drugstore on the corner near the playground – Arlene called to say we're low on Kotex for tomorrow; she's got to be at the college until late tonight, can't pick it up. Let's do that before anything else.

She lowers her voice, smiles at the baby and says, We're going out, Joey, going out, going out, going out.

Ok, but I think we should go to another place – let's get it at that big new supermarket; they have a grand opening sale and no Janes shop there yet. It's not far.

Hold still one more second, Joey. Just *one* more second, this – pin – is – just – about – *closed*. Yes! All done! She lifts Joey to his feet, walks him along the hall and talks louder toward the kitchen. Ok, good idea.

They bundle Chloe, Sam, and the bag of food into Claudia's old station wagon. Denah holds Joey on her lap.

As Claudia pulls away from the curb, she asks Denah, Are you still mad at Gert?

No. I'm not mad at her. It's just that I realize I don't like her, which is a different thing altogether. I thought I liked her when I first joined the Service, I thought we'd be friends, but now that I know her better, I can't like her. I don't know why *you* do – actually, I don't know how you *can*, but I'll try not to be obnoxious about it.

They laugh. They've discussed Gert before.

Sam says, I have to go.

Ah. We'll be stopping very soon, can you hold it?

I'm trying. I'm trying to hold it.

Denah and Claudia look at each other – Claudia scans their position and says, Gas station. Just a few more seconds, Sam. She pulls in. As she turns off the ignition, Denah slides Joey across the front seat toward Claudia and gets out. She zips Sam into the restroom. When they come back, she leans into the back window and says to Chloe, How about you? Want to go?

No. Yes. Chloe starts to work the door handle, stops. No.

Claudia laughs. We'll need just one of those – which one do you think it'll be?

Chloe visibly considers, then says decisively, NO. I'm waiting. I want to go at the new place. Sam climbs back in and says, I'd have waited if I could.

Ok then. Denah gets into the car, takes Joey back onto her lap. Claudia turns and looks back over the seat, admonishes, You two sit down back there. And, in a voice like a robot: *Everybody please remain seated while the vehicle is in motion.*

Then she puts the car in gear and says, I don't have the same reaction to her bossiness that you have.

Denah says, Oh, it's not about bossiness – if bossiness bothered me, I couldn't love *you*! She's a phony, that's the problem, she's a phony. I know you think she's being careful, thoughtful, helpful – taking care of people, but I think she's manipulative and dishonest.

Ah. *Now* let's talk about something else.

Fine with me. Have you seen *Cabaret*?

Please. Who do you think you're talking to? Isn't that a movie for grown-ups? I still haven't seen *Willie Wonka* – I think that one came out about a year ago. Lucky for me, I read the book.

Some people said it was too scary for children, too weird, and the Gene Wilder character is sardonic and mean – have you heard that?

I haven't, but that's foolish – first of all, it's based on a story by Roald Dahl. Kids love his stories, and he's *always* mean. Children understand mean – they can deal with mean. Children even understand sardonic, though I suppose I wish that weren't true. I wish *I* didn't understand sardonic – oops, here's the new place. Almost overshot that drive. Good thing they've got balloons all over.

Chloe yells, Balloons! Balloons! Balloons! Joey, instantly filled with her excited energy, says Buh, buh, buh!

Chloe, come in with me – we'll find the bathroom and the Kotex both. Claudia pushes the food bag under the seat to keep it out of the sun, and gets out of the car.

Then Sam says, I want to go in too.

Denah hoists the baby onto her shoulder and says, Let's all go in. We'll scope out our new Service resource, your community's newest commercial enterprise.

3. *Jane Sets Up A Full Service Service*

Allie is at her gynecologist's office, sitting on the table in an examining room, wearing one of those little gowns with fluttering ties that don't keep it closed. She's reading a tattered copy of *National Geographic*, dangling her bare legs while she waits.

A doctor enters, closes the door, says, Hello, Allie. How are you? I didn't expect to see you here for at least – he looks into the manila folder in his hand – another six or seven months. What's going on? You ok?

She puts down the magazine, smiles, says, Hello, Doc. Actually, I'm fine. I wanted to talk to you, so I made an appointment, to be sure I'd get at least fifteen minutes. I only put on the gown so I wouldn't have to explain anything to your nurse.

Her manner is not typical of women in these gowns, these offices. But he barely notices because he's used to her; he's been her doctor for ten years. He's about that much older than she is, in his mid-forties.

He puts the folder down and says, OK, so this is a consultation, not an examination. What are we talking about?

Allie, in a slightly lower voice, says, I know you're one of the more enlightened OBs in Chicago – she grins at him – that's why I let you deliver my kids; you know that. Also, we've always been candid in our conversations, even about difficult subjects. And I think I can trust you to keep this conversation confidential.

Uh-oh. Difficult subjects. Confidentiality. He sighs. Is this political, Allie? He smiles, sits down on the little rolling stool. You're such a pain in the ass. That's a medical condition. *Is* this political?

Hello. This is Jane.

What isn't? Philosophically speaking. Right? Look, Doc, I know some people who're helping women get abortions here in town.

He shoots a look at the closed door.

I'm not talking about the mob, the bad guys, the vultures. I wouldn't waste our time and my husband's hard-earned money talking about that. These are people doing skilled abortions in clean, supportive conditions, helping women who don't have the kind of money it takes to go out of town, to travel. That's *most* women, Doc, and you know it. I know you do. And I know that when it's legal, you'll do it yourself. But right now, it's not, so what you can do, what you *could* do, is this: do what's called for, by Hippocrates and your own conscience. You could agree to be a backup, a phone consultant, an emergency resource – for if and when such a thing is needed.

The doctor's surprised – but not stunned; he knows who she is.

How is my helping criminals going to be legal?

You're not helping the abortionist, you're helping the woman. Maybe she's running a fever, maybe she's passing clots, maybe she had an induced miscarriage with a five month fetus and she needs a clean-up D&C. Maybe she's hemorrhaging.

You said these people are "skilled"? Doesn't sound like it.

I'm talking about the tiny number of emergency cases. Come on, you know the story; nobody has a perfect record. Plus: nobody in your business has control over what the patient does when she leaves the office – what her home life is like, whether she gets enough sleep, whether she's getting punched around, all of that. And – what if *your* office had to be a motel room, had to be a bedroom in a different apartment every week? What if, because good medical practice has been made a crime, the practitioner can't stick around to be the backup – like you can? This would be rare, Doc. Maybe one call a month, maybe two. And if you can recommend any pals you think would be equally trustworthy, there'd be more back-ups to share the responsibility.

Here's how it would work: Let's say a woman has a D&C, let's say she was nine weeks, let's say her health was borderline. Two days later she starts bleeding a lot – so she calls me, tells me all about it. I call you, tell *you* all about it. You tell me what to ask her, what to tell her; you prescribe something. Maybe – very very very rarely – you call your office or the hospital, tell them your patient is coming in and you'll be there in thirty minutes. I bring her – or a friend of mine does. That's how it'd work. I know it's not ideal. We're not talking about ideal here; we're talking about real, the real lives of real women dealing with this stuff every real day. And you know that.

Jesus, Allie, this is heavy! How'd you get into this?

You don't ask me that. You don't ask me anything that's not about the medical condition of a woman or girl who needs help – help *you* can give, if you choose to. I have to protect people who are risking arrest and imprisonment to do this. I have to protect you, in fact, and you are definitely on a need-to-know basis. So. Do you want some time? Should we talk more, outside office hours? We can meet at the lake, at the park, or at my house. Come over for a sandwich, sit in the kitchen with Steve and me. Or come for a ride in the pickup with us – it's pretty cool, you know, driving around in the truck bed, lying down and looking up at the sky.

Steve knows about this?

Of course he knows about this! He's taking care of the kids while I'm doing it!

Hello. This is Jane.

Oh, Allie. Can't I just organize a march? A demonstration? Get signatures on petitions to make abortion legal? Couldn't I just chain myself to the fence at the capitol building in Springfield?

You can do all of that – except the chain thing. We need you to be available.

* * *

That night she tells Gert about her recruiting success before the meeting starts, while everybody's kibitzing, before they get down to business.

Mandy's saying to Rachel, Last Thursday there was an epidemic of vomit! Seemed like *every*body threw up! I've never seen that before – you know, there's maybe one in a week – but this was memorable. One woman says, I had breakfast before I came. I know I wasn't supposed to but I was so hungry I just ate everything in sight. Is that ok? And then, later, she says, I think I have to throw up. I wanted to smack her – it was not a sisterhood moment.

MaryAnn thinks Mandy's wrong: Yes, it was! It was! If not for sisterhood, you *would* have smacked her.

Ok, good. I'm relieved. But she was just the beginning – less than an hour later, right in the middle of a D&C, another one says, I have to go to the bathroom right now. Stop. I just have to go to the bathroom, and then I'll come right back.

Rachel says, No wonder the regulars like to put everybody to sleep.

Denah says, Yeah, then another one shows up at the place – she doesn't say this at the front, or to the driver – waits until she gets to the place – and *then* she says, I don't feel so good, should I do it anyway? So naturally we say she should think it over and decide for herself, and we give her a little private corner to sit and think, and then she says she wants to do it, and when we're done she throws up all over, and we have to slow down the whole schedule *again*, to clean up that room while she's crying, moaning – I'm so sick, what a mess, oh I'm sorry, I'm so embarrassed – and all that. What a scene *that* was.

Allie raises her voice just enough and says, We have some really important business to discuss tonight, so let's get started. Gert and I have some things we need to tell everybody.

Sandy says, in an undertone to Lucy, Well, that's real different, isn't it?

Gert stands up, as if to speak more formally, and says, You know we've always called the abortionists "Doctor," whether they're MDs or osteopaths or naprapaths – what*ever* they are. And we all know dentists and veterinarians do abortions, as well as curanderas in the barrio. And we know some are better than others.

Lucy calls out, Yeah, and some doctors are no good at all, including way too many gynecologists. We *do* know that.

MaryAnn says, Look, is there something going on here? Let's hear it – get to it. C'mon, you two, get to the point.

Allie stands up. Ok, I will. Jake is not a doctor. He's not a gynecologist or obstetrician; he's not even a veterinarian. He was assigned to the medics in Korea and learned to do abortions from the docs in the army. He's got no initials after his name. He never even went to college.

- *Oh, shit.*
- *Well, that's that.*

- *No way! He's good! Too good to lose.*
- *That must be where he got that Asian-looking tattoo. When I asked him about it, he just said, Long ago and far away.*
- *Well, we can't use him anymore. We can't take women to a guy we know's not a doctor. Bad enough it's illegal to begin with!*
- *But lots of the women like him – he's so nice to them.*
- *And he's good! He doesn't fuck them up, he doesn't come on to them, and we can count on him. We can trust him.*
- *Yeah, right, we can trust him – call that trust? He tells us he's a doctor when he isn't?*
- *Did he ever actually* tell *us he was a doctor? Or did we just assume it because that's what he was called, introduced as?*
- *Oh, who cares? Let's think about it – our whole scene is illegal anyway – let's remember that: we're all criminals, so what difference does it make, if he's good?*
- *We've got a relationship with him now, and it's working really well – I say we keep him.*
- *If Jane keeps working with him, I quit. I can't lie to the women.*
- *Who says we have to lie? We tell them the truth.*
- *They won't want to come to people who aren't doctors.*
- *Yeah, right. They'll decide to have babies they can't afford to have, babies they've already decided they don't want, because Jane's guy doesn't have a framed diploma hanging on the wall of a Michigan Avenue office. Are you kidding? Have you been paying attention to what goes on here?*
- *What our guy has to be is* competent *– as well as safe, cheap and good to the women.*
- *That's what Jake is – well, ok, he's not as cheap as we want, but we got him to come down some and we're working on doing that again. From the women's point of view, and given our set-up, it's do-able.*
- *Obviously. We have a full list every week.*

MaryAnn waves her arms in the air. Hey! Wait! *Here's the thing, think about it, here's what really matters about this: if he's* not a doctor and he can do it, that means *we* can do it. That means anybody who's got brains and skill and training can do it – *that's* what this means.

• *Oh my god! She's right! Talk about your goddamn medical mystique! What have we been howling about for the past three years? The docs have all the knowledge, they don't share it, they mystify their practice, they infantilize their patients – this cuts through all of that!*

• *I bet lots – maybe most? – of the guys who do this aren't docs. I never thought about it before – what a joke! I never doubted them, even though they're all criminals.*

• *Like us.*

• *Stop saying that!*

• *We can learn from Jake and do it all ourselves. We can do everything!*

• *What makes you think he'll teach us? He's in it for the money, after all. Why would he train competition?*

• *He's taught us a lot already – half of us are doing longterms now.*

• *Look, I'm not saying it's stupid or evil, I'm just saying that I won't – I can't – do it. If that happens in the Service, I'll have to leave.*

• *Will we be able to keep getting new Janes if we do this?*

• *What will the women think if we're the ones doing it? What'll we say to them?*

• *We tell them we learned, just like you learn anything. We tell them they can learn too, if they want. We already tell them they can join up and counsel; this is just (laughter) – this is just more work!*

• *You know, I respect this, I respect you all, I see this is the way it's going. But I don't think this is right, and I'm not going to be part of it. I'm going to quit the Service.*

Hello. This is Jane.

Claudia says, Look, we all know, in the history of this group, how every time something shifts – policy, I mean, or action, some people quit – they decide they don't want to do whatever the new thing is, and they leave, like when the Service changed from only referral to counseling & referral, and when we added Janes as drivers, started using places and fronts that *we* arranged instead of the abortionists. Handholding and assisting, once Jake let us in. Longterms. So some women quit – they quit because that change, that new thing, whatever it was, was not ok for them.

She stops talking, looks around, thinks about those who want to leave, stop now, quit.

She goes on: But isn't it also true when new Janes come in, at the next orientation after the change, it's not a concern? I mean, the new women come in on whatever terms we have *then*; they make *their* decision based on what we tell them we do, whatever we – the Service – *is* in that new version. Most of them don't even know it was ever different, they just come in at that moment in time, accepting it as given – that's what the Service is to them, and they want to do it or they don't. That's how I came in – I learned the Service *was* what it was when I joined. That will always be true.

Denah says, I say we do it.

All right, Denah. Yeah. What Claudia says is true, but I think a lot fewer women will come in for *this* – this is really *radical*, really *criminal*.

Denah looks at this Jane, a woman she is fond of, a woman she has laughed with. She says, Kathy. Kathy. If you think what we've been doing all along isn't really *radical*, isn't really *criminal*, you're deluding yourself – if you think the reason cops stay away from us is we're not *really criminal*, you are on some other planet.

Allie, who is smiling at Gert with secret-knowledge eyes, says, I like this idea.

And Gert replies, Yes, I think we should do it.

At these words from Allie and Gert, most of the Janes exchange looks. They know the two leaders have now decreed what will happen. Some of them wonder if it's already happening. Wouldn't be the first time Allie and Gert have taken action and brought it to the others afterwards. In fact, some Janes think there's stuff they never bring to the group at all. That would not surprise Denah, or Claudia. They look at each other intently.

Gert pivots the conversation: Also, we need more doctor contacts. Anybody seeing a new ob-gyn, I mean, one you feel good about?

Mandy says, I met a doctor at a party last week, and we actually talked about the possibility of abortion becoming legal soon; he thought everybody would learn how to do it if that happens – which I took as a good sign. But I don't know his last name – he was just John at the party. You know how that is: Mandy and Fred, this is John and Lisa, blah blah blah.

Gert says, Oh, great, Mandy. That's not *too* much less than helpful; thanks.

Allie leans in front of Gert to tell about her doctor, his reluctance trumped by his politics – and his trust in her. Everybody cheers.

I've got a friend who's in medical school – he may be meeting some good people – and I can ask him tomorrow night, MaryAnn says.

Sandy says, I go to a GP I love – what about that? Do we have to care what their specialty is?

Allie says, No – but then it gets tricky. He's gonna look suspicious if he starts admitting gyn patients to his hospital – one in a year, maybe'd be ok, but a few, even a couple, could get him in trouble.

Lucy remembers the guy she met at Mary Jo's cousin's birthday party – she liked him; he was really funny. His name surfaces in her memory and she says, Anybody here know Lance Malley? He's been around a few years – oh! wait, he's at a Catholic hospital. Shit.

Arlene says, What about Charak Sharma? The guy who started doing abortions when he was an intern – he'd meet the women at that pink motel out by the airport? He's a sweetheart. By the time the Service really got going he had his own practice – did his own patients and a few of our women too. You know who I mean? I saw him at the big peace march last year; he was walking with that medical contingent – they all wore scrubs, remember? They're the guys who palled around with Concerned Clergy at the Take Back the Night march. They were cute: the men's auxiliary to the women's liberation movement. I'll find him.

Allie says, Be careful! Do it carefully, that *finding*.

Arlene puts her hands up as if she were being stopped by the sheriff in a cowboy movie and says, Yes! Yes, *carefully*, of course! *Very* carefully.

Gert says, This sounds good. All of this sounds good

Sons and Lovers

The door to the bathroom is covered with tigers. Panthers sprawl nearby, yawning their fangs open. The big cats scream, they claw red blood, the drops of blood are shaped like tears. Some have green eyes, some red. The cats are small, medium, large and very large; the biggest panther, blue white eyes and rose red tongue, might be two hundred dollars in 1971.

Through the dim window, from out on the sidewalk, Norma thought Dwayne's place could be a barber shop, with its old magazines on the low table next to a rumpsprung couch in front and three big chairs with mirrors behind them, further back. But when she opened the door and got past the couch, there were the walls, covered in flash.

Some places show each guy's stuff on a separate wall, but at Dwayne's the walls display the basics, the ones everybody does. There's a book of originals next to each chair, drawings and photographs with a list of prices, and estimates for custom work. Norma stood at the counter and slowly turned, eyeing each wall's panels.

In one corner are cartoons, some familiar and innocent. The Disney dwarves are here – three hundred fifty dollars for seven in a row or pay by the dwarf. Grumpy costs the most, all those lines in forehead and eyebrows, but Dopey's smooth little face and long sleeves go for only forty dollars when he's six inches tall.

One wall has all the women, twenty-five to two hundred dollars, mostly naked pinups from the forties: ass up, legs spread, cupping their breasts and sliding long scarlet fingernails over their own variously tan, yellow, purple black, chocolate brown, red or white thighs. Norma expected this.

The only naked man is Satan, whose bright red penis is a hose, or a spear, or a cowboy lasso. Sometimes he holds a trident of fire and flakes of flame spark off his horns; his thighs are furred, his nipples pierced, his tongue a sharpened spade. To get the devil and some hellfire carved into your skin, you pay at least fifty dollars.

The nearly naked man is Jesus, who hangs on his cross looking sad or looking dead, his loincloth bright white against peachy skin and gloomy sky. There is no hair on Jesus' body, but the thieves are darkly hirsute, and the skulls are shaded blueblack with stormy green highlights. You can get Jesus alone, or with Golgotha and the skulls included. For the devout with a hefty paycheck, there is a Deluxe Crucifixion: all three crosses, one or two Roman soldiers, Mother Mary weeping and the Magdalene tearing her robe while the heavens open above the head of the Christ. Thick torsos can sometimes accommodate one or two apostles.

Legendary at Dwayne's place is Lenny LasVegas, who got the Deluxe Cru on his back, and when all the scabbing was gone, came back to get a Deluxe Nativity on his chest, belly and thighs: three wise men with camels and various livestock surrounding Mary, Joseph and the manger with the star above and a few humble shepherds, out of proportion but subtly colored, below. These two jobs were done in installments, a series of sessions that took eighteen months and cost Lenny over a thousand dollars. Norma heard about Lenny later.

Lenny LasVegas may seem unusual but there are many tattoo legends. Dwayne's favorite is an ancient joke he likes to tell when he's working; he tells it as if it actually happened out on Clark Street: Three women of the night (he does use that phrase) are talking about johns with tattoos. So Tenny says this and Concha says that, and then Maybelle says, Listen, you talk about tattoos, I had a guy once, he takes down his pants and the letters on his dick spell out LITTLE. The others laugh, but she holds up her hand and says, Well, yeah, that was funny, but when he got going, what it really said was Little Rock, Arkansas, Gateway to the Southwest.

Dwayne loved that. His standing offer, much repeated, was that he'd do it free for any guy who was cocky enough. Then he'd laugh and say, *Cocky enough – get it?* Norma was amazed at this, when she finally heard him say it. He was, she knew by then, a sweet man.

And Dwayne was a sweet man, truly. He liked to do lavish vows, love ribbons on arms and chests. While he shaved out the space carefully, he'd ask questions about the person whose name he was about to ink in: Peaches, Susie, Jonny-boy, Sarah, Jose Diego. He wanted to know their favorite color, their favorite movie, whether they liked pizza or tacos or hot dogs, if they lived in the neighborhood.

When the name in the ribbon was MOTHER, Dwayne would ask: You send her flowers on Mother's Day? What kind? Then he'd hang a couple posies from the ribbon ends. Word on the street was, if the guy in the chair – laid back, feet up – said he didn't send flowers to a living mother, Dwayne pressed a little harder on the downstrokes of the M. Norma didn't know any of this the first time she walked in, but it made sense later.

Dwayne's own mother calls him at work every day, at his insistent request. She does it because he asks her to, but she prefers to keep the conversation short.

Hello Mama! How is it with you today?

Dwayne, I just came back from the market. Today I got some chocolate covered doughnuts, the kind that come in a long box with a cellophane window in it. Those doughnuts are shiny – their frosting looks like the coating on an ice cream bar but it's a little wavy. Have you seen them? The inside's yellow cake, and it's even moist – heaven only knows what they do to keep it that way. Oh, see how your ideas have gotten into my head! I'm sure they're just fine.

Yep, I'm sure they are.

Honey, even the speed-out lines were busy today, so I got a lot of reading done. I read that JFK is visiting Jackie. He's been seen by several people, so there's no doubt. I wonder what he thinks about that stubby old man, that Greek. And I wonder what Jackie thinks about poor Marilyn.

What makes you think she knows?

Oh honey, *ever*body knows. We know, don't we? Now, I only wanted a couple doughnuts, but there are eight in this package. I'll just put these others in the freezer for another time; maybe G will have some when he comes over.

Sounds like a good idea, Mama.

Now you take care, Dwayne, and I'll see you later.

Bye, Mama.

Rosemary Clara Larken never had any more children after Dwayne. She always said she wished she could have got him some brothers and sisters, at least one little sister for him to take care of like her brother G had taken care of her, but she'd always say, things just didn't work out that way. She had Dwayne when she was fifteen, on a bright blue October morning in 1935. His daddy went west before he was born, just picked up and walked out the door after breakfast one Tuesday, Rosemary told her son, without so much as a kiss goodbye for the wife he called Little Girl. She explained that some men did this, many men had in the hard times. He never did come back. She told Dwayne his daddy had gone to be a hobo, a word Dwayne liked to say when he was little. Uncle G called the disappearance of his sister's husband a good riddance to bad rubbish. When G moved up north, he took Rosemary and her boy with him to Chicago.

Dwayne doesn't remember the first place they lived because Uncle G found something better pretty quick. That old G is just as smart as he is tough, Rosemary said, and you know how tough he is; we're proud he's family.

Smart, tough, and lucky, Dwayne decided later, when he realized his uncle missed the whole war, never went overseas, and had a real good job being a janitor in a big apartment building on Lake Shore Drive. Dwayne understood now that G had supported him and his mother in those early years, the hard years before he'd made himself into a business and had other men working for him.

They lived all together at first, in a basement apartment at G's job; then he got two other places, one for him and one for them. He came to visit often, and when he left he'd say to Dwayne, Gotta go now, boy; your Uncle G's got things to do, places to go, people to see.

Dwayne remembers clearly – even now, coming into the seventies – the years his mother worked at the front counter of the L-Stop Laundry & Dry Cleaners on Wilson Avenue, taking in the clothes, writing out customers' slips, bundling shirts into canvas carts with rattling wooden wheels, and sticking the slips into them with great big metal pins. When customers came for pick-up, she'd read the number on the pink slip and search back through the racks, sliding the wire hangers along until she found the matching white copy. Then she'd bring their clothes to the front, where she put shirt boxes on the counter and pulled a long flat paper bag down over the clothes on hangers. That was before we had all this plastic, honey, she'd say now. She tied up the hanger necks with a bit of white string, like what bakery ladies snapped off with their knuckles on the knot. This'd be tighter with wire, but the wire's for the soldiers, she'd say then. Dwayne's memory of WWII is sparse, but he does recall being allowed to keep his own ration book on a little shelf beside his bed.

The best part, Dwayne thought when he was a boy, was ringing up, pushing the keys to open the drawer on the cash register and making change. He told this to Norma when they were telling each other about growing up. Rosemary taught him to count back so he could do it too: like if somebody's bill was $1.20 and they gave her two dollars, she would take the bills and lay them on the register ledge, ring open the cash drawer, and count out a nickel and three quarters into the customer's hand, saying, All right now, that's one twenty out of two: here's twenty-five, fifty, seventy-five – and that makes two dollars. Thank you so much. She always said Thank you so much. Then she'd put the two singles into their own section of the drawer and push the drawer back in.

She told him it was important to always leave those dollar bills out there until she was done so the customer couldn't say, Hey lady, I gave you a five, or something like that. Not many would do it, honey, but there's some that would, and even the nice ones could make a mistake, so you have to protect yourself. Dwayne wanted to grow up to have a job where you could take in cash money and count out change, saying, Thank you so much to a whole lot of people.

Rosemary's job was a treat in the winter, she told him, because the laundry and cleaning machines were right there in the back and kept the place warm. 'Course, in the summer, which was just generally Hades in Chicago, no denying it was awful hot and sticky in there, but summer wasn't long and winter was, so she wasn't about to complain, she'd generally say. This was a real good job, she'd tell her boy. Get old enough, Dwayne, you might could get you a job in the back, or out on the truck, drive all over the whole north side of this city.

But that didn't turn out to be Dwayne's real good job. He started to hang around a tattoo joint on Broadway when he was eight or nine years old. He looked in the smeary windows, got a clear view occasionally when somebody held the door open to keep talking, and soon learned that the man nearest the door was Jerry, so that was who he talked to when he walked in the door and up to the counter one day and said he wanted to learn. The place was crowded on weekends, when soldiers and sailors had more passes, but business was good all the time. Jerry turned out to be the boss, and he gave Dwayne a job sweeping up, taking out the garbage. Meantime, Dwayne drew on paper, on the inside covers of his schoolbooks and on sidewalks with bright colored chalk he swiped from the kindergarten room on his way out of school at three o'clock.

In those years, Dwayne told Norma in impressive detail, he lived with his mother in the apartment G found them in Uptown, a one bedroom on the top floor of a skinny three flat. They had the landing of the creaky wooden staircase right outside their kitchen; Rosemary put a chair out there in the summertime. Dwayne slept in the bedroom and Rosemary slept in the front room. Only Dwayne's room and the bathroom had doors; the kitchen and parlor doorways were arches with a point at the top – a pretty shape, Rosemary thought. She hung a bright cloth up at the entrance to the front room, pulled it shut at night and tied it aside with a red cord during the day. Their kitchen was big enough for the table and chairs G brought over in 1947, saying, Look at this, Ro. Don't these look like they coulda been carved back home? Now you got a little bit of Kentucky right here in Shee-caw-go. The chairs had curvy tops and they matched the table; they all had high backs, and two had wide arms, so they were good for listening to the radio.

The apartment was not far from the tattoo place on Broadway and about six blocks west of Stewart School, where he learned to read and write and do arithmetic in the classrooms of teachers much older than his mother. Three of these were named Miss Leary, Miss Lloyd and Miss Lorraine. His mother remarked on all these L's and told him that when she was a girl back home she'd had a teacher named Miss Prince who got married and changed her name to Mrs. King. Yes she did, Dwayne, for real now.

Miss Lloyd had been his teacher in third grade, and taught him to do more fractions than usual – even decimals – because he was, she said, a bright one, sharp as a tack. That's what she told Rosemary at Open House. Rosemary sat in one of the little desks with a stack of Dwayne's school papers in front of her. He just wants to make pictures, but he can do lots more than that when we encourage him, Miss Lloyd told her. We must always encourage him.

Miss Lorraine, the eighth grade teacher, was his favorite. She would say, Wonderful! Wonderful! to whatever he told her. He'd say, Miss Lorraine, I have to write my book review on *How Green Was My Valley* because when I got to the library, *The Grapes of Wrath* was out. And she'd say, Wonderful! You'll like that book, Dwayne! Or he'd tell her he couldn't join the band because he had a job after school when they practiced, and she would say it: Wonderful! Good for you, Dwayne! That takes gumption! Thing is, she would say it like she meant it, like she really did think it was Wonderful, whatever he said to her. Her big dark eyes would open bigger and her mouth would smile just as big and her whole face would look like she really did mean it. He never thought she was phony, like Miss Leary, the first grade teacher who called everybody Sweetheart but never thought a one of them was sweet and they knew it. But they all felt good when Miss Lorraine said, Wonderful!

The first time Norma watched him work, when he was done, when he had sprayed the tattoo and was getting ready to cover it, she looked straight into his eyes and said, Wonderful! That was a moment, he thought now, recalling it. That was a moment.

Some people remember tragic or funny or surprising things, but Dwayne remembers mostly what he thinks of as regular everyday life. Like, when he was a boy, his mother never made him eat anything he didn't want, but he had to choose from what was already there, in the icebox and cupboards. By the time he was in high school, he'd usually choose a can of soup and add things to it, like apple slices or celery or crumbles of toast and cheese. Rosemary would say, Now, Dwayne, there's things already in there, they make it so you don't have to put in even any water. I know, Mama, he'd say, but the things already in there are too soft. She always had some cans of soup up in the cupboard, with the sugar and salt and baking soda; she called these things staples. When he asked her why she called them the same name as the little metal paper fasteners, she said, Well honey, I guess I don't know; that is what they are though.

Raising Dwayne, Rosemary'd been careful about food, and one result was, except when he was in the army and had to eat what *they* had, he was pretty much always robust and cheerful. He'd learned from his mother to put apples, carrots or something green along with the leftover macaroni, the ham or tuna sandwich in his bag when he packed his lunch to eat at the shop. Then he'd gone beyond that, beyond her, to think about things like this new idea of complementary proteins and, later, organic vegetables.

Every morning Dwayne makes a drink in the blender, putting in brewers yeast powder, raw egg yolk, apple juice and whatever fruit's in the kitchen: peaches on the verge of going bad, bananas like his Uncle G prefers them – nearly black, so soft they're almost liquid inside the skin. These're still good, Ro, he'd say, taking them out of the garbage while Rosemary rolled her eyes at Dwayne. Dwayne, now, doesn't go that far, but he says they're not ripe if they have any green on them; he says they're a little hard to digest until they're nice and brown. When he pours the dregs of his drink out of the blender, he runs a little water into the glass canister, swirls it around, and drinks it. That way he gets as much of it as possible, and wastes almost nothing.

He does that every morning, standing at the counter by the sink, looking out the window at the corner where the #8 bus stops. When Norma had occasion to be there in the morning, she was impressed by, but did not choose to share, his methods.

Rosemary had surprised herself by developing a ferocious sweet tooth once Dwayne was grown, and in the past couple years she'd thrown over her own baking – apple crisp and berry cobblers – to focus entirely on chocolatey things. She explained this conversion by telling how her daddy, who died before Dwayne was born, had picked up a taste for chocolate over in France, in the first big war. Clovis would say, Rosemary has explained more than twice, that over there they eat chocolate with little spoons out of teeny tiny china pots: chocolate thicker than syrup but not thick as pudding. That was something, Clovis has been quoted many a time as saying. If her daddy was alive and in Chicago, Rosemary told Dwayne, he'd be purely delighted to eat chocolate all the ways she did now.

Here's something to know about Dwayne (Norma seems to have known it from the start): He's not like the wall flash at his place; he's not disneyfied and he's not skanky. He's not what people expect when they come in; he's more complicated than you think he's going to be. He never argues with customers – unlike Vince, his shop's first owner, who had a list of strict rules. Vince wouldn't put a rose on a woman's bicep. Maybe on her leg or belly, tits and ass for sure. That's where you put roses on a woman, he'd say – red roses. *Mmm, ok, maybe pink or yellow sometimes, but red is best.* He wouldn't do anybody above the collar line. *They're not gonna blame me for that when they sober up.* And he played only classical music on the shop's radio. *The needle stays on that station; it's art for art, see?*

Dwayne, when he took over, had only one rule: He wouldn't do anybody underage. They could watch, the young ones, so long as nobody put a needle to their skin in his shop. But everybody knows he breaches his own rule if they're military. Those are the only kids Dwayne doesn't card, children wearing clean uniforms and shiny shoes, boys with cheeks as smooth as Dick and Jane and Baby Sally, who come in with the fleet at Navy Pier and take the train up to the north side, or get a pass and come down to the city on the bus from Fort Sheridan. Dwayne thinks if you're old enough to ship out, you can ship out with pictures. Norma's anti-military, but she's impressed by Dwayne's treatment of those kids (boys not really so much older than hers) and she likes it that he won't obey a law he can't respect.

Vince sold the shop to Dwayne when tattooing surprised them all and started to attract new kinds of people. Vince got a little famous then, and wound up out in LA, opening a place he called Twentieth Century Skin Pictures. After that, on the couch in front of the window and across the street at the newsstand under the tracks, everybody said Vince was doing some big names; there were rumors of Cher.

But the shop stayed pretty much the same when Vince left; Dwayne liked the arias and sonatas just fine. He did add one thing, though. He put up a sign that said: *The difference between tattooed people and people without tattoos is that tattooed people never ask you why you're not tattooed.* He'd seen that in a parlor out west when he was coming home from Korea, and it made him laugh. He still smiles when he looks at it.

Tattoo here. Hey, Mama – how are you today?

Dwayne, I'm just back from the market. I thought I'd try something new, a bag of chewy chocolate cookies – but they're awful! The picture on the bag looks like they're going to taste good, like the ones we got downtown that day at the old market, remember? But they're not like those cookies, they're gummy. They're making my cough worse, too.

Rosemary coughed just then, as if to offer an example.

Hearing the cough, Dwayne winced and started to say one kind of thing but turned it into another. Instead of the cough, he focused on the cookies: Mama, if they're no good, you should throw them out.

Oh no, I'll eat them; you know I hate to waste. But I am truly disappointed. Well, today the cashier in one speed-out lane was calling for a price check, and the other one was closed, so I got in a regular line, behind a family with a cart full of soda pop and nothing else. But even though their cart was full, the checkout took less than a minute because they had seven cases of the same thing. All I could do was scan the headlines, no stories today.

So you got no report for me? All right then; I'll have to go without.

No, except you can be sure I won't buy these awful cookies again! What a sunny day! I hope you aren't so busy that you never get outside, Dwayne. Bye, now.

Bye, Mama. He stood for a moment at the phone, looking at something inside his mind, then turned back to his chair.

Sometimes Dwayne could hear himself sounding a little bit like Vince, telling a first time customer, You'll be back. Dwayne knows what Vince had known, watching the way someone would run a finger slowly around the tattoo, rapt. He would say that to the ones who stared at a fresh tattoo, who didn't want him to cover it with a bandage because they were stunned in love with what they'd done.

He kept all the Japanese flash that Vince had left – the geishas and samurai, some classical shoulder work, Mount Fuji – and he brought in Cal, who was good at it. Dwayne himself was basically US of A. Unlike Vince, who'd been to art school, Dwayne had learned on the sidelines at Jerry's place when he was a kid and then picked up a few skills and ideas his two years in Asia. When he got out in '56, he came back home and got a job at Vince's place, where he learned the rest – mixing pigments, using the autoclave and the gun, widths and speeds – and added all that to the natural talent Miss Lloyd had been so worried about. He was willing to hang around, clean up and do the shitwork for other guys so he could learn. He read tattoo magazines and *National Geographic* at the library. He hadn't realized there was so much to learn about tattooing, but he liked learning it; he got ideas, and when business heated up again in the sixties, he used them.

When Vince said he was going, Uncle G fronted Dwayne the down payment for the shop, and Dwayne's been paying him back more quickly lately. Business slowed down some after Korea, stayed level until the mid-sixties, took off again with VietNam. Less predictable was this popularity prompted by rock stars and politics, whirlwinds that blew women like Norma into the shop.

That day Norma first came in, she was wearing a three piece suit and carrying a briefcase. It was late fall, still sunny but already cold, and she had a bright scarf around her neck and shoulders. She unwound it as she studied the walls. She started at the bathroom door, examined the cats, touched a small panther with the tip of one finger. She looked at everybody's flash like she was judging a contest. Dwayne had a red ceramic Kwan Yin on his work table, and in his book a purple-robed Guadelupe with stars in her hair. Women liked those. And Norma admired them, but they were not what she'd come for.

She wanted a double-winged dragon with scales of gold and faceted emerald eyes. She wanted it between her breasts, seven inches long. She had wide set breasts, she argued, and her breastbone was pretty flat, so that should be simple enough to be well under a hundred, she haggled with him at the counter. The men on the couch by the door listened while Dwayne showed her basic flash and made some suggestions. Finally, they agreed to make it five inches, leave off one set of wings and settle on sixty-five dollars. Then they walked through the curtain at the back.

Dwayne used the back room for customers who needed to undress. Not just women; men used it too. He didn't want anybody out in the open like that, didn't want to draw an audience for bodies, only for pictures.

Probably because Norma had done her bargaining at the counter and jockeyed for a good price, she became a conversation topic at Dwayne's. The regulars called her the dragon lady. You gotta wonder about the deal that one cuts between the sheets, some guy on the couch would murmur. She's gotta be women's lib, probably carries a gun in that briefcase. Then Dwayne would say, That woman has three children, Harry, all three of 'em just a few blocks from where you're sitting right now, talking bad about their mother. Two big boys and a baby girl not even in kindergarten. That's all she talked about. Then Harry, or whoever it was that time, would press his lips together and cut his eyes at the other men on the couch.

Only Dwayne knew her name, Norma Frances Crosby; she'd introduced herself before she took her shirt off in the back room. Her driver's license had another name, Norma F. Sheridan – he saw it when she opened her wallet – but he made no comment; lots of people got tattooed at Dwayne's using names not the ones they were born to.

Norma was taller than most women of her generation, so she was used to being regarded with suspicion and fear by men. She'd been thinking about this since she hit five foot three in the sixth grade, before women's liberation was on tv. In other ways, she liked to remind herself, she was just regular, and this comforted her. Dwayne had no idea about that at first.

The conversations he had with Rosemary were pretty much all the same, but they satisfied Dwayne. When the phone on the counter rang, whoever answered would say: Tattoo. Dwayne puts the accent on the first syllable, Stevie and Cal both hit the second. Stevie's closer and usually answers; when it's Rosemary, he and Cal have been told to get Dwayne no matter what he's doing.

So the phone rings and Stevie says, Tat*too* – like a cartoon sneeze. And then he says, Yes m'am, I'll get him. Hey, Dwayne. Then Dwayne says to the sailor in his chair, Just sit tight now; I'll be right back.

Dwayne, honey, I know you're right, what you say about eating dairy, but I did go straight to the big freezer today, and got a pint of that pink Cherry-Chocolate. Even though it's cold outside, that was what I wanted. If they'd had ice cream bars in dark chocolate I'd have gotten one, but they only had vanilla insides with milk chocolate outsides, and you know I never have liked those.

It won't hurt having ice cream every little once in a while, Mama – that old moderation thing, right?

Yes. The checkout lines were so long today that people were talking to each other while we waited, all of us strangers, not like how it usually is. One thing everbody said was how we always choose the wrong line, all of us. And speed-out lines always seem to move slower than the regular ones, when it's supposed to be the other way. Now, isn't that the strangest thing? Well, it's a fact of life, we all said so. In my line some people said the bank does the same thing, and the post office too. When are they going to do something about it, was what we all wondered.

Dwayne sends a smile and a small lift of his chin over in the direction of Stevie's chair and says into the phone, You need an assistant, Mama. I send young Stevie on all our errands to avoid that very problem. Stevie and Cal both laugh.

Well, with all that talk, honey, I only saw one story – but it was a ripsnorter. It said that Marilyn and James Dean came here to Illinois, not to Chicago but over west to Pecatonica – 'member we drove through there that Sunday on the way to the river? Marilyn and Jimmy came to see one of those spirit women, like the one who sits in that storefront with fringe, over by the Wilson el. The woman in the story was out there, in the back of a real small café. She promised she'd try to find out if there are movies in heaven.

They say Marilyn was wearing that beaded dress she wore in *River of No Return,* and when she got chilly Jimmy gave her his leather jacket. But oh, Dwayne – there was a fight! Some of the people who came said Marilyn and Jimmy weren't really there, and started a big argument that ended in a ruckus, and now the café owner can't get the damage paid for because the insurance won't believe how it happened. Isn't that the way of it?

Yep, people will fight about anything if you give 'em a chance.

Now Pecatonica folks are all taking sides: some are blaming the spirit woman, some are blaming the café owner, some are blaming the non-believers, and some are even saying it's Marilyn's fault. That poor girl is still so misunderstood.

But I have been talking way too long. I'll hang up. You got somebody in the chair, don't you? You go back to work. I'm about to eat that ice cream, right down to the last little chip of chocolate. You be good now, honey, and I'll see you later.

Bye, Mama. He smiles. There's no cough this time.

In the spring of '71, a new shop opened south of the Loop, and in summer Jerry's place on Broadway brought in a fourth chair. Everywhere now was like the forties. Creased regulation trousers lined up next to rainbow patched denim bellbottoms, and the work in the chairs alternated between eagles and peace signs. Both sides liked the cartoon weed labeled *I Love MaryJane.* They never tried to hurt each other at Dwayne's place, even if they screamed and spit and bareknuckled downtown, or kneed and shoved each other off the concrete piers between Fullerton and North Avenue. At Dwayne's they took chairs side by side and listened to Bach.

And it wasn't just them. There were guys from the coffee shop, the grocery, the gas station, the discount carpet store and the army-navy surplus place. Crowds came by for Cub games. A headshop had opened on the block in '68, around that time the Jefferson Airplane came to town, and that brought in the trade. Daily action in and out of the turnstiles at the Belmont el stop was steadily growing.

Dwayne was scrupulous with equipment, and treated the men at the other chairs with friendly respect. He was a good boss, had a good mind for business; he paid attention to the trade. Dwayne couldn't have predicted what would happen to tattooing at the end of the twentieth century, but he was on the case in the fall of '71. He told Cal and Stevie: There's more people who went to college now, see? A lot of these people think about art. We gotta think about what they think about. And the women – the women! You see what's happening here? Women! What have we got for them? Think about it, boys.

While they thought about it, Dwayne answered the phone: Tattoo.

Hello, honey. I surprised myself today, and got a little box of cupcakes. These have teeny sugar daisies right on top, but someone had enough sense to make the frosting and the cake both be dark chocolate.

Ah, your favorite – twice!

Today I was behind a young woman whose little one, a baby in the cart, kept trying to reach all the candy. That's why they put it there, those devils, to entice all the children and exasperate their mamas. So I talked to the baby and read aloud from the magazine covers to keep it busy. The mother told me gracias when they left; I said, *de nada*. She smiled at that; she'll never know those are just about all the Spanish words I ever did have.

Oh now, Mama, I think you've got more than that – I recollect you could do a little business in Spanish at the cleaners.

I guess, over there, but you know I never have gotten good enough to say whatever I wanted to say – only what I had to say. You know what I mean. But listen, honey, those cupcakes are good. The cake's a mite dry but the frosting is real fine, almost like fresh, like from that good bakery over on Lincoln Avenue, the Germans. Well, you go back to work now, Dwayne, I haven't got another thing to say. I believe I'll take a little nap.

That's a good idea, Mama. Bye.

Because of the women, Dwayne is always on the lookout for flowers; he thought the majority wouldn't want the kind of work Norma got. He believed most women love flowers (well, maybe not stone butches), so he built a collection of roses: he had tight buds, flowers half open, and full blown blossoms in red, yellow, pink and a new blend, fiery orange – all with long green stems, pointed leaves and a scattering of thorns. They priced out from thirteen dollars to full body costs, depending on size and difficulty, and separate ones could be made into a bouquet. We can put 'em together just like a florist, Dwayne would say.

He added sweetpeas in clusters, pansies in pots, bunches of iris tied with a ribbon and one design each of tulips, lilies and gardenias. That last one gave him the idea to put in a head and shoulders portrait of Lady Day; he thought lots of Chicago musicians would go for that. He encouraged Stevie and Cal to copy popular images, and to experiment.

Cal, who had two years of art classes at a city college, copied Georgia O'Keeffe's desert bones but drew his own blossoms. About O'Keeffe he said: You know, her stuff ain't necessarily better than mine; they just recognize hers, is all. Stevie did daffodils, and specialized in vines, mostly ivy and morning glory. These definitely attracted women, who also liked the bracelets of Celtic knots in green and gold men had begun to wear around their wrists and ankles. Stevie did car emblems too, including classic hood ornaments; Cal did cartoons of all four Beatles.

Some of the oldtimers objected to the presence of women, but Dwayne argued that he couldn't be turning money away, could he? The men said sure, he must like them a lot; he was the one who got to hold onto those juicy tits! He had women back there with their panties off, for chrissake! Harry said, You guys put your hands all over these women's legs, make them squirm with that needle. Dwayne shook his head and clicked his mouth to one side in a sharp little sound. Then he'd say: You fellas. You fellas. Lots of these women come in here are *mothers*.

So the regulars got used to the women, and the men who walked in cold got over it when a woman sat down in the next chair while they were getting Born to Run, Born to Kill or Born to Die lettered into banners on their chests and shoulders. The men lay back when Dwayne, Cal and Stevie cut Blue Demons, Flying Tigers and Semper Fi into their skin, or copied a picture of the Dead or the Doors off an album cover. And they squinted the corners of their eyes when a woman in the next chair toughed out a rising cobra, its wide open hood just at her kneecap, the needle on bone making her wince – but not cry.

Privately, Dwayne thought about how even the tough ones were nothing like Carlotta, who'd been on the carny circuit and used to come to Vince to get her portraits of US presidents touched up. He noticed that a lot of the new women showed up in pairs and groups, not so much with a man, like before. But he liked to say about these new ones, when they'd first come in to watch, Look what's happening here. You see what's happening? They'll stay and they'll pay.

Making his point with emphasis, the dragon lady came back at the turn of the year, bringing with her another woman and a little girl. My daughter wanted to know where I got my dragon, so I brought her in to see, Norma said.

Gracie, this is Dwayne; he's the one who drew my dragon with an electric needle and colored ink. Dwayne, this is Gracie. They looked at each other. Dwayne nodded a greeting and lifted up his book for the child; she took it with both hands.

Are there sharks in here? Like those ones? Gracie pointed to the wall beside Stevie's mirror, where the primary motif was sharks swimming open-mouthed, displaying stylized rows of razor-edge teeth. There were sharks with hammerheads, tiger markings and thresher tails, some long and thick with "Mako" or "Great White" stenciled in calligraphy along the curved lines of their tails. I don't want sharks. I'm not going to look at those ones either. She made a little turn, tilting her face away.

That book has my own pictures, Gracie. No sharks.

She carried the book over to the front window, sat down on the couch next to Harry and began to turn the thick plastic-covered pages.

This – the dragon lady said, gesturing to the woman next to her – is my friend Sylvie. She wants a tattoo.

Dwayne turned to the new woman. He raised his eyebrows and gestured with both arms, indicating all the flash to choose from.

I want a star, she said. A pale blue star – one of those, over there. She pointed toward a section of the back wall, a small heaven of suns, moons and stars in multiple versions and colors. The stars were drawn with five, six, eight and more sharp points, in gold and silver, flaming red and cool blue, set into constellations or burning alone.

I want just one, here. She placed the palm of her hand flat at the top of her chest, below the opening of her collarbones. Right here.

We can do that easy, Dwayne said. Take down that set and show me which star you want.

Sylvie pulled the tacks out of the wall, brought the drawing to the counter and put her finger on a single star with eight points, its heart the size of a silver dollar.

You want it colored like this? Silverblue with some green, and that pale turquoise shading?

Yes – I want it just like that, please.

Ok then, I can do a straight trace. That star'll be twenty dollars. Cash money, in advance. Have a seat, lady.

As Sylvie unbuttoned the top four buttons of her shirt and settled in, Gracie called out: Where's my mama's picture? This dragon has more wings but my mama's doesn't. Why? Where's my mama's more wings? Can I watch Sylvie?

Not this time, honey, Norma said before he could answer, taking Dwayne's book from Gracie and putting it back on his shelf.

It's ok with me if it's ok with the lady here, Dwayne told her.

Thanks, but she can't stay – it's almost time for playgroup. Nodding to Sylvie, she said, I'll pick up Carlos from your mom, take them both, and be back when you're done.

Norma turned to Dwayne. You can answer her questions another time, thanks, but before we go, will you show her the needle, please? Buzz it a second so she can see it move?

The man in Stevie's chair grunted. The hell is this, Kiddyland?

Dwayne's head turned at this and his mouth opened to reply, but in that moment the phone rang, Norma took Gracie's hand, and they headed for the door. Dwayne signalled to Sylvie he'd be just a minute and reached for the phone with one hand as he returned Gracie's small goodbye wave with the other: Tattoo.

Hey there, honey. Today I felt like those little teeny chocolate chip cookies, the ones you used to call chippers, the ones small enough to put in your mouth whole but you could eat them in bites if you want to? I like to drink milk with 'em, so I got a little school-size carton of 2%. I do know skim is better for you but I can't abide it – you know it really is more like water than milk. I'd still be drinking whole milk if not for you, Dwayne, so don't you be upset.

I'm not upset. I appreciate you giving me credit for my good advice.

I had that mean cashier today, the one whose sweater always smells like cigarettes. I never can see why anybody'd be mean to people they don't even know, can you?

I'm sorry to say that I can, but no reason you should, Mama.

You know, there wasn't nothing but Martians in the paper today, it was hardly worth reading.

This must be your day off, then, Mama.

Some things maybe, but see, I have eaten all my cookies, and I didn't time it right – ran out of milk too soon. Sometimes I can make do with a can of grapefruit juice, but there's none in the pantry or fridge. I won't go back to the market though – I had a lot of that coughing, and it about wore me out.

Mama, I'll come bring you some juice; I can be there before five.

No! No you don't, Dwayne. I want you *not* to do that. I want you not to do that a whole lot more than I want something to drink for those cookies. This is what G calls *in*consequential – purely *in*consequential. She breathed a thick sigh and coughed once. You are a good boy, Dwayne.

All right. All right, I won't do it. I will see you later, though. I'll see you later.

Yes, later on, honey. Later on.

Take care now, Mama.

He hears her cough as they hang up. The coughing isn't going away. Dwayne knows that, and so does Rosemary.

Outside, Norma hustles Gracie down the block to the bus stop, where they sit on the wooden bench to wait for the 22. Gracie's humming, mostly inside herself, and Norma's thinking fiercely, as always.

Norma turned 34 that January; she'd been born in 1938, when some people in Chicago had hopes for the end of the Depression, and she was raised up into middle class education and expectation. At this moment, sitting at the bus stop, she's working on her situation. Her situation is serious.

Ronny Sheridan is in real estate; she married him when they both were 21. She went to St Scholastica and was, her mother says now with anguish, *just an ordinary girl, a nice ordinary girl.* She's being blamed by her parents and his, with the priest sicced on her like a Doberman. It feels to her like everybody in the parish has enlisted in the shaming and blaming of Norma Sheridan. It's as big an event at St Gregory the Great as the summer carnival. Oh, she's exaggerating, but these people are not merely irritating in their disapproval of her forcing a good Catholic husband to get a divorce. There have been major consequences. The judge is a friend of her father-in-law, a man who misses Father Coughlin on the radio.

Norma loves her kids. Gracie is 4 now and the boys are 7 and 10. Ronny Jr is the elder; the family calls him Ron2, and they spell it Rontu on birthday cards and cakes ("like a robot, yeah!"). Jack is the younger, named for her father, who calls his grandson Jacky the giant-killer, Jacky the beanstalk climber.

Norma used to love Ronny, she thinks. She remembers kissing his naked belly in bed, but this memory is grotesque now. She wants to have her life not be about her marriage – before, during or after it. She insists on noticing and mentioning, and she keeps on talking about, the changes: children grow and change and turn into people they weren't before, and their mothers do the same thing.

She told Ronny she wanted to stop having kids after Gracie. Ronny said they didn't have to worry because he was doing so well. She said that wasn't the point. He asked, What other point could there be, Norma? He blamed her attitude on Vatican II and, of course, women's lib.

The biggest problem seems to be that Norma has become a photographer. Ronny was amused and pleased when she took such good vacation snapshots, even when she took classes at Columbia College. But he was puzzled and then angered by her interest in photography as a thing she wanted to *do*; she never but he always in their fights would call it "a career." He said, If you wanna take pictures of the kids, fine. Fine. You should do that. But if you're thinking of turning into a real photographer, I mean somebody who actually *is* a photographer, you can forget it. If that's what you want, if that's what you're thinking, you can stop thinking it right now – I mean, not married to me, Norma, not in this marriage you're not. What do you think, you could be famous like, like, what's his name in the papers, the turtleneck guy with the Polack name? Or no, no, wait – it'd have to be a *woman*, right? Some lady photographer, as if there are any. Well, I mean it, Norma – you can just forget it.

She didn't say any more when it got to that point. Instead, she began doing real estate interiors, getting jobs from people she'd met through Ronny. The connection amused her. She did some of this for free, just to have it appear in magazines and the color pages of the Sunday papers, to build a portfolio – gold coast apartments and corporate offices. And she did occasional parties, saving the money in a bank account he didn't know about; she used a co-op darkroom she found in *The Reader* classifieds. She did all this without telling Ronny, squeezing it in between the parts of her life that were approved by the family and the priest.

But that didn't last long, only a few months – it was too much to keep secret and it was exhausting, the tension of having to remember all the lies. He thought she was having an affair, unable to imagine she was lying so she could be and do what she'd told him over and over she wanted to be and do.

Now that they were divorced, she did whatever jobs she could – even weddings – to make the rent, feed Gracie and support her own work, which right now was candids of her kids and shots of the lake. Sometimes she thought about movies, moving pictures. But for everything she saw through the lens, she wanted to make what film people call a "still," a picture of one small part of the whole moving world, held still.

Norma lost custody of her sons to their father because, as her father-in-law's friend the judge said, given her way of thinking – her insistence on giving prominence to *her work*, given her being, he could see, under the influence of *feminism* (he snarled the word as in her in-laws' kitchen she had heard him snarl *communism*) – she was not capable of creating a home life that would nurture small boys into strong men.

Ronny said, when they met with their lawyers, that he didn't have to worry about Gracie because she was a girl; it was the influence of women's lib on his sons he worried about – he'd seen in the paper where psychologists were calling it *emotional castration*. That was what got him. He didn't know Norma was meeting with other women to talk about their lives and help each other live them. All he knew was, his boys were in danger of being raised by a woman who wanted to take photographs, develop them herself, show them in galleries and publish them in books.

She got the dragon tattoo right before they went to court, an icon to keep her strong. It was a mark of defiance. But then Ronny took the boys, so the dragon became her symbol of enraged fortitude, strength beyond the human, what she thought she'd need in the coming years. Now she has the boys for two three-day weekends a month; on one of those weekends, Ronny takes Gracie. This means the children are all together with their mother for three out of every 30 days. Sometimes in between, Ronny and the boys pick up Gracie and they all go to Ziggy's for hot dogs.

She thought Ronny and the judge believing she was a danger to the boys was so obviously absurd that her lawyer could get the custody decision set aside, could overturn it somehow. At first and for a while she could not imagine that insane arrangement would stand, despite stories she kept reading about what was happening to women in courtrooms all over the USA. It was so stupid, she kept saying, and besides, Ronny had never taken care of any of them, never so much as made a peanut butter sandwich, couldn't remember what grades the boys were in, didn't know their teachers' names.

But it was Norma who was stupid, stunned into a temporarily lower IQ. Her lawyer, who was not stupid, not stunned and had seen much worse, assured her that if she attempted to fight for the boys she would lose Gracie too. When she was able to think again, she knew this was true. Norma knew that not so long ago – even now in some places – Ronny could have had her locked up. She could have been put away for her *unnatural* behavior.

Ronny pays a little child support for Gracie. The judge came close to denying this, suggesting that the earnings from Norma's *career* should go to pay for her female child, but her lawyer argued that she was still a novice photographer, that their claim was reasonable, and that there were several positive precedents, unlike – for instance – the decision to split up the children. The judge grumbled but acceded, finally saying girls cost less than boys and Norma shouldn't expect Ronny to spend as much on Gracie as he did on Rontu and Jack.

During these discussions, Norma sat without moving, rigid. The only thing alive in her mind was a set of variations on one repeating theme: It's good the kids aren't hearing this… good they don't make the kids listen to this… at least the kids will never hear this. And when it was over, her lawyer guided her out into the courthouse corridor and propped her against the marble wall behind a column until she could breathe naturally. When her body lost its stiffness, she started to slide down the smooth wall; then the lawyer helped her over to a bench.

Norma used to bite her fingernails, but made herself stop six months before she got married so she could have long nails and wear silver polish for the wedding. Now she bites the skin around the nails, sometimes until it bleeds.

Norma waved through the shop's window sometimes, on her way from the train. Twice that winter she sent more people she knew; one was a man from the darkroom co-op; when he got there, he told Stevie that this photographer chick he knew had sent him. And Dwayne realized he could remember what she looked like when she wasn't there.

After getting the star, Sylvie brought in Denah, a local writer who wanted a leaping dolphin at the curve of her shoulder. Then Judy, who's in Norma's women's group, had Cal trace the ten of cups from the Waite deck onto her hip. Stevie told Dwayne there are 78 pictures in every deck, so maybe they should keep one at the shop. And more women came in, saying they'd seen the star, the dolphin, the dragon or the picture from the Tarot.

One day Norma came in alone, pretty late. She was wearing jeans, boots and a hooded parka; it was snowing thickly, fat wet flakes. Cal and Stevie were both working; they nodded to her. Dwayne was sitting in his own chair, looking at line drawings of trees and leaves.

She came behind the counter and stood in front of him. I'm glad you're not busy. I need another tattoo, Dwayne, but this one's just for pretty, you know? No symbolism, no metaphor. I need to give myself a gift, something lovely. Here's the thing: I never wear bracelets – when I try, after a few minutes they start to bother me. I like the look but I don't like the feel; I always take them off. So I want a bracelet I can't feel. I want a chain of flowers around my arm, and I want the flowers to be all different shapes and colors. I've got thirty-eight dollars – what can you do for me?

Dwayne stood up and opened his notebook; he quickly sketched several little blossoms, hooking them loosely together with curly tendrils and leaves. This one'd be yellow, this one red – I'll come up with some orange; we can use blue, I've got some purple mixed, all the leaves'll be green. And I think it'd look better with some repetition, Norma, not with every one completely different – we can do it with color or shape or both – but you want them to work together, to complete the design, see what I mean?

Norma looked at the sketch, looked at Dwayne. There were rosebuds, daisies and asters; not one blossom was bigger than a dime. Yes. You're right. Of course. I don't want each one to stand alone, I want one design, integrated: a bracelet, not a set of samples. We're making art here. She pulled off her parka and tossed it over to the couch, sat down in Dwayne's chair and rolled up the sleeve of her flannel shirt.

They talked about design for a while, how your first idea may be only an opening and maybe gets dumped once the work starts; about how making pictures with a camera is different from doing it with a needle but, fact is, they both spend a lot of their time making pictures. As he shaved clear a ring of skin on Norma's left forearm, Dwayne asked, How're the kids? You know, I see all these friends of yours, I see that little Gracie, but I never have seen those boys. What, do you think this place'd be a bad influence on their little boy heads? Does their daddy have tattoos?

Norma's arm stiffened in his hands. Are you saying I think it's ok to bring Gracie here but not my boys? That I'm following some kind of rule here? Some rule about gender? About kids and gender? Is that what you're saying? Her voice got lower and tighter with each word, and ended in a whispered rasp.

Dwayne let go of her arm and leaned back. Hey! Hey! Wait a minute! I'm not saying anything that should make you spit tacks. I just wondered. You told me about your boys when you first came in, but you haven't said a word about them since, so I'm curious; that's all. That's all's happening here, Norma.

Well, they're fine, she whispered. They're fine. Let's get going on this bracelet.

Cal and Stevie exchanged the kind of look that comes up from under your eyebrows, made silent whistles with their mouths. Stevie said to the guy in his chair, So! What about those Cubs? Already lookin' good down in Florida, right? Cal started singing "It's Too Late," switched to "Fire and Rain," then dropped into a hum.

Dwayne worked steadily for nearly an hour. He said nothing the whole time except Turn your arm now please. Norma said nothing, period. Tears came to her eyes when he did the underside, the soft inside skin that never toughens. But when it was done and she raised her arm, turning it and bending her neck to look at each small flower, she smiled a real smile at him and said, It's exactly what I need, Dwayne. And it's really good. I'm so sorry I hissed at you. I'm really sorry. There's things making me crazy right now. I'm sorry.

No need to say it again, Norma. I do believe you're sorry.

Everybody was done at about the same time, and everybody went for a beer. Cal made it happen. Norma, he said, we ought to at least buy you a drink, since we don't give you a percentage on all the business you're sending us – whyn't you come out with us?

Sylvie had Gracie at her place 'til 8 that night, so Norma pulled on her parka, put on her mittens and said, Yeah – you guys can thank me formally tonight. Let's go. She put up her hood.

It had snowed steadily since early morning, and people had been shoveling. Some streets had parking spaces dug down to the asphalt, their empty car lengths staked out by kitchen chairs with brooms balanced between them, blocking the cleared area. Some had chunky blue salt crystals scattered over the cleared out space. Stevie said, No Chicago jury would convict you if you killed somebody who took the parking space you dug out and marked; no judge would sentence you if they did.

Norma looked out of her hood at him. Don't talk about judges, ok? Their boots crunched on the packed sidewalk snow.

She'd never been to the dim bar near the corner of Racine and Belmont, but the men were obviously regulars; the bartender greeted them by name. Norma lived a little further south and east, in the rapidly gentrifying neighborhood around Grant Hospital where bars had begun to be called taverns again. She and Gracie had a three room coach house behind a Victorian on Dickens; it was tight, but they could walk to the lake, the lagoon, the zoo and the playground in five minutes, and six different buses stopped within a few blocks of their tiny yard. She was lucky there, Norma knew; she figured she had maybe three years before she'd be priced out of her lease.

She was happy to think about ways to see herself as lucky; it didn't happen often. Last weekend, when the boys were with her and Gracie, Rontu objected to the nicknames she had always called them – Cupcake and Pumpkin. At first she thought, Ah, here it comes; he's gotten to an age when endearments like that are embarrassing. He's probably thinking, What if some other boy, someone from school, heard me call him Cupcake?

When she was setting out their sleeping bags, he said, Mom, you make us sound like food. I don't think you should do that. Assuming she knew what he was thinking but wanting to hear him explain it, Norma smiled, asked why.

Because what if somebody thinks talking like that makes you An Unusual Mother, even more Unusual than you are already? Then maybe Jack and me won't be allowed to come over. I think you should stop. Even the baby, you call her Sweetiepie-pie, like she was a Twinkie or something.

That night lucky seemed pretty far away.

Cal drank Bud because, he said, he actually liked the taste, and Stevie did too because Bud's all about the Cubs and so is he. Dwayne wasn't much of a drinker, as it turned out, but when he did have a beer – like that time – it wasn't Bud.

Because Bud's on all the signs, and I don't like that, he says. I guess I resent advertising; that's just how I feel about it. He ordered Dos Equis. Uncle G had introduced him to it a few years ago when he was dating a Chicana chef and learning about the differences among varieties of chile peppers.

Sometimes when Dwayne orders a beer, Stevie tells Norma, he'll get an older Milwaukee brand, maybe Schlitz, just because he's sympathetic – he knows it's going down in popularity. Dwayne's like that, he says.

Ah, no, come on; that's not it, buddy. It's more like I want something different, something I've picked out myself. That's a small thing, but it's important – you know what I mean, don't you, Norma? I bet you do. She nods. Yes I do, Dwayne. I think I do.

Soon after that, Dwayne and Norma started going out. First time, she and Gracie stopped at the shop with a little white bag of bakery cookies, and while Gracie was handing them out – one with blue jimmies for Cal, one with red jimmies for Stevie – Norma leaned in and said quietly, Dwayne, let's go for a walk or something; you and me, I mean. How 'bout this Sunday, when you close early? If it's not too cold.

Dwayne blinked and took a breath – not audibly, nothing so dramatic, but he did breathe differently for a beat or two.

They decided she'd meet him at the shop at five, then they'd go for a walk and decide what they wanted to do; they'd just be loose, see what would happen.

That day, she took Gracie over to Sylvie's after Carlos' nap. Much as Gracie loves Sylvie, they all know Carlos is the main attraction. He's younger and tolerates Gracie's condescension, so they literally – their mothers say – play nicely together. When Norma got to the shop at five, Cal and Stevie were gone, but there was another man there. He'd shown up an hour before, surprising Dwayne, who hadn't seen him since the army. He's Sunnyside Turner, a skinny guy from Oregon who re-upped in the fifties but got out when VietNam started getting bigger. I could see what they were gonna do, you know? I wasn't into that.

When he sees Norma, he says, Hey, I don't want to mess up your plans. But Dwayne looks at Norma and Norma says, Hey yourself, don't be silly – come on out with us. It's not like we've got only two tickets for whatever we're doing.

They went over to a café on Diversey. Dwayne had a dinner salad and Norma had potato pancakes and Sunnyside had biscuits and gravy with string beans. The men talked about the army, about Korea, about war. It was conversation Norma'd never heard before. She used to ask her uncles, who'd gone to WWII. There was one who had the bucket of blood insignia on his jacket, who'd been at the Battle of the Bulge; his answer was always, Sweetheart, you don't want to know. Most of the uncles had been in Europe, but there was one who'd been in the south Pacific, and he got so mad at that movie in 1958 that he stood up and demanded his money back – Got it too, he told her. But that was all he told her. None of them ever said anything real. Sunnyside and Dwayne were talking real.

Since high school, Norma had tried to keep up, to count the wars the USA had been in since she was born. The easy ones were the Second World one and the Korean one that Dwayne and Sunnyside and her cousin Lonny went to (like the uncles, Lonny wouldn't talk). VietNam was the longest one so far, not counting the Cold War, which was different, but still. She had a feeling there were some little ones she'd not noticed or forgotten, and this embarrassed her, even though nobody knew. She told about Lonny: a javelin got stuck through his leg by another soldier and he was sent home. Aunt Cecile was ecstatic.

Norma asked the two men how that might have happened. They said, both at the same time: Hey, he was lucky. Sunnyside said, See, you practice a lot, it's part of the training, sometimes you have what they call war games. Like teams in a school ballgame, where you're playing against each other, it's not really enemies because you're all on the same side. You use real rifles with real bayonets and real javelins – but not real bullets. That kind of thing, one GI hurting another one, yeah! That happened. Truth is, Norma, sometimes one GI would kill another GI. Some guys went crazy from that. We didn't know what we were doing; we were just kids, and we were raw. I tell you, Norma, we were truly raw. Javelins – you know what they are, right? Spears, really, they're spears. And your cousin, he probably was too close to a guy with bad aim, is all.

They talked about how, when they killed somebody, they would sometimes be glad and sometimes be scared. Dwayne said, Like when you're little you say, He started it! He shot at me first! So it's ok when you shoot back, see? And if you don't, you'll die sooner than you want to. That's how you learn to think about it – when you think about it. Some guys liked it. Sun, remember that guy Karl, the big one? He liked it. He had a good time out there, all us laying on the ground with dirt up the legs of our pants and in our mouths. Yeah, big Karl was happy to be there.

They talked about going on leave, and never understanding what Asian people were saying. Listening to people talk there was like listening to music, wasn't it, Dwayne? – you knew it meant something, but you didn't know what, so it was like music without words, like jazz, or what you got on the radio in your shop.

Once when Dwayne was on leave in Okinawa, he bought his mother a wooden music box; black, lacquered and polished to such a high shine it gives back reflections like a mirror. It has a little house, some trees, and a creek with a bridge carved on it, painted, raised and inlaid with abalone on the lid. It looks like jewelry, Rosemary said when he gave it to her. She was surprised to hear it play "Three Coins in the Fountain." Now why would they make such a pretty box all their own way, and then put somebody else's music in it? Dwayne said he didn't know why, but pretty as it was, that song surely was what made him buy it. Hearing that song was like hearing his own language, even without words, and he needed to hear it over there, he told his mother. It was his language and it was saying something the army wasn't saying.

I played it a lot before I brought it home, Mama; I was thinking I might wear it out and have to get another one to bring home for you, but it was all right.

Sunnyside showed up at Dwayne's shop because he was passing through Chicago, hitching across the country to see his sister and her kids in Pennsylvania. He's thinking she needs him to help out; she has four kids, had a husband for a while but not now, and it's rough. He'll get a job there. That's his plan. Dwayne says that sounds like a good plan for Sunnyside, for the kids, and for his sister.

Norma agreed, and she got an idea. Her idea is that maybe Dwayne could take care of Gracie sometimes when she has night gigs. She's getting jobs she can't schedule during playgroup hours and she's been asking Sylvie too often. She's got other friends who take Gracie sometimes, and Dwayne could be one of those. Gracie likes Dwayne – he talks to her like she's a real person. What if she brought Gracie to the shop and Dwayne took her home with him when he closed, or brought her home and put her to sleep? This could be a good plan, Norma decides, like Sunnyside's plan is good. He and Dwayne walk Norma over to Sylvie's, where Sunnyside says goodbye; after sleeping on Dwayne's couch, he'll be hitching out in the morning. Dwayne says, See you soon, Norma.

The first time Norma decided she actually could leave Gracie with Dwayne – she had kept her version of the Sunnyside plan to herself for several weeks, telling herself she was right about Dwayne, asking herself if she was right about Dwayne, laughing at herself for thinking so much about Dwayne anyway – she took the plan to her women's group. Some of them gave her a hard time, jumped all over her: Hey, are you nuts? How long have you known this guy, ten minutes? Who is he, really? Wow, Norma, I'm surprised at you!

Sylvie slid to the front of her chair and had already opened her mouth and begun, Well, you know, I – when Norma blurted out, He feels right to me; I trust him, and Gracie's comfortable with him. We've been spending time together, remember? Do you think I would risk Gracie with someone I don't know? Gracie knows Dwayne, she knows who he *is* – you know what I mean? Are you worried because he's a tattoo guy and you think he's some kind of outlaw? You all thought it was cool when I got tattooed – you said you did, anyway. Some of you met him – you took your shirt off in his shop, Judy – what do you think? Helene, is this because you think tattoo people are dangerous? Is that what this is about? If it is, that's ridiculous. Jesus Fucking Christ, he's responsible, he's dependable, he treats his workers with respect; he even loves his mother – talks to her every day on purpose. And he's better with Gracie than her own father is. Her grandfathers too – those are the men I need to worry about.

The room was quiet for a second or two in the wake of that rush of words. Then Andrea said, Wait a minute – some of us haven't even said anything yet. Judy said, The day I went, there was a woman who told me she liked the guys who did the work but the vibe from the other customers was sinister – and something about the couch. I think she said "The sofa is sinister" – whatever that means.

Helene said, Oh Norma, we're just afraid for Gracie. I mean, what the hell have we been talking about every other Wednesday night for two years? Our brothers, our fathers, our husbands. So many of them turned out to be no good one way or another – not good enough, anyway. Are you sure he's good enough? How can you be sure?

I didn't say I'm *sure*, Norma said. For that very reason, all our Wednesdays, I wouldn't say *sure*. I don't say *sure* about anything anymore. But I think this is a good thing. I think Dwayne is a good man. And – she looked around the circle with a cockeyed smile – we all know what *that* means. A couple women smiled, one laughed. Sylvie said, Not only are they hard to find, but this one, this good man, is gonna do childcare! Or, he's about to be given the opportunity to do childcare; let's put it that way.

Norma had already run through the objections raised at the meeting and answered them in her head; she'd needed to hear it from the others, needed to have it examined. By the time she finally did ask him, she and Dwayne had walked all over the winter beach from Grant Park to Rogers Park with and without Gracie, eaten pizza at Due's with the kids one early spring weekend when Rontu and Jack were with her, and seen *Cabaret* and *The Godfather*. They had slept together in her bed and his.

The final point for her, the time her decision solidified like the edge of Lake Michigan in February, was when she explained to Dwayne how to prepare Gracie's favorite food: Kraft macaroni, cooked with butter and milk like the directions say, but without the powdered cheese from the box mixed in.

Instead of doing that, Dwayne, you take a square slice of orange cheese out of the pack in the fridge and break it up into little bits and make a ring of them around the edge of her plate. Better yet, let Gracie do that part, she loves to. And give her lots of time, Dwayne; don't even heat the noodles until you think she's nearly done. When she is, pour some of the hot macaroni out of the pot into the middle of her cheesy little sunflower. Then you can mix the orange powder into the rest of the noodles for yourself – if you should care to eat them, Mr. Clean. Gracie'll swoosh her noodles around, pulling in the little cheese bits one at a time. They never melt, but they get real slippery. Give her a spoon for this.

I bet you'll like the way it looks, Dwayne. It's a design thing as much as a food thing – you'll see. Now, sometimes, Gracie'll want tuna fish. She likes it the way Ronny's mother Genevieve makes it, mixing a spoon of Miracle Whip in with half a can of tuna and adding tiny peas. I never met anybody else who uses little peas to make tuna salad, but since Gracie tasted the way her grandma does it, that's what she wants. It should be tuna packed in water, not oil.

Encouraged by his silence or unable to stop herself, Norma went on: For a snack, she likes to put a slice of that orange cheese on top of a slice of bread that's been spread with ketchup. She likes the cheese to fit on the bread, but she likes all kinds of bread so that's where you can sneak in something healthy – some stoneground thing that'll make you happy, Dwayne. Sometimes she'll say: Make it pink, please. That means she wants you to mix the ketchup with Miracle Whip. Genevieve told her this makes Russian dressing.

Through all this, Dwayne said nothing, simply nodded his comprehension. When she finally stopped talking, he said, I think she could be eating more vegetables, and more fruit. Even in the winter there's ways to do that, Norma.

She smiled, nearly laughed. Hey – buy it, bring it, you have my blessing. Let me know what works.

One time, when Dwayne and Norma had gotten further into whatever their relationship was becoming, he agreed to pick up Gracie from playgroup because Norma was working an eighteen hour day, three different gigs. But on that day, he realized he wasn't going to get away from the shop as long or as soon as he'd planned. It was spring break at DePaul, Loyola and the city colleges, and the chairs were full. People were waiting; they were signing up on a clipboard Cal put out on the counter, going out for half an hour and coming back to check the list, like at a restaurant. And on top of that, one of Chicago's notorious spring snows was starting up.

At five o'clock, Dwayne finished waving a small flag across a bicep and ran out to get Gracie. Instead of bringing her back to the shop, he drove up Broadway and took her to his mother's apartment. When they got there, Rosemary had just prepared a green salad, opened a can of tomato soup, and was getting started on devilling up some hardboiled eggs.

Mama, this is Gracie; she's Norma's girl – Norma's working, a real long day. Gracie, this is my mother, Rosemary. Mama, you will have to forgive me. Work today has gotten out of hand, and I can't get her home in time to eat right. I'll call you later, but I don't know when that'll be. We have so many people waiting, the couch is full; you've never seen so many customers. *I've* never seen so many.

Gracie, you accept my apology, don't you? She nodded. This'll be fine, won't it? I'll be back to take you home for bedtime, and Norma will get there while you're sleeping.

Rosemary bent down to help Gracie take her mittens off and untied the knotted strings of her hat. Together they peeled down the sleeves of her parka. Rosemary arranged the damp mittens, small parka and wool hat on the radiator. Gracie sat down on the floor in the hall and pulled off her boots with two intense little grunts. She stood up and looked around.

Rosemary said, You're just in time. This is perfect; come back here with me, child.

Dwayne kissed his mother's forehead. Rosemary smiled and murmured, She looks like a sweetheart, this one. I see how it's all going, Dwayne.

She and Gracie walked back to the kitchen as Dwayne closed the front door. She handed Gracie a bowl to mix together mayonnaise, mustard and smashed up hardboiled egg yolks. You know, Gracie, deviled eggs are my brother G's favorite, so we're making a big batch tonight; we'll put the ones we don't eat, the extra ones, in the icebox for him.

Gracie had recently begun to make jokes in the style demonstrated by Rontu and Jack when they visited. Yeah! They'll be *eggstra,* she yelped, *get it?* She told Rosemary, I have brothers too. They're older'n me, and Rontu's older'n Jack. Dwayne knows them. They don't live with me either, so Norma and I could make devil eggstras for them and put them in the fridge at our house. My brothers live with my daddy because the judge said. I have a play baby brother, Carlos; he's more baby than me, so I teach him things. Where does your brother live? Is he older than you? I think older brothers are a good kind to have.

Next morning at home, Gracie crawls into Norma's bed. She and Dwayne both have sealed eyelids, sunk deep into skin puffed out like biscuit dough. They keep their eyes shut as Gracie pushes between them and starts talking. Last night, they'd both been way too tired to talk.

Gracie tells about the red soup, the green salad and the yellow deviled eggs; she tells the eggstra joke, says that Rosemary's brother G is Dwayne's uncle G, and that Dwayne's mother is tired, not like she used to be.

She coughed but she doesn't *have* a cough. She has a music box I could open myself if I was careful. I *was* careful. And she has a *radio*. We were sleepy when Dwayne came to bring me home.

What? Where were you, Gracie? Where was this? Norma is now awake, her eyes cracked open between their crusted lids. Didn't you go to the shop?

Dwayne sits up and pulls the quilt to his neck, covering Norma and Gracie completely. It was too busy, too many people, too much going on to have Gracie there, Norma. I took her over to my mother's place. Rosemary gave her supper. I came back for her later. A lot later. She was asleep when I got there. We didn't close until nearly ten and the snow made everything take longer. It was crazy. I didn't have time to tell you.

Norma slides up next to him, her back against the headboard. *Tell me*? Don't you think *ask me* is more like it? Don't you think you should have *asked* me if you were going to do something like that? Change our plan, take her out, leave her with someone *else*?

Gracie climbs out from between them. Are you fighting? I don't want fighting. She gets off the bed, goes out, closes the bedroom door with a careful click.

A scene like what we had going at the shop is not for her, Norma – lotta bad talk, some bad behavior. You know? I didn't want her there and my mama's was the first place I thought of. It was fine. I was in a hurry, I didn't have time to call, wasn't even sure where you'd be, but I knew it would be fine. What would you have done if you knew, left your job? I mean, I took her to my *mother*, Norma, not to a stranger.

Oh, well, that's ok then, right? The fact that you know she's a good person, that makes it ok? When I don't know you've done it – I'm out there thinking I know where my daughter is, but really I don't? Where do you get off doing that? And what the hell do you know about this? You're no mother. You're not even a father – not that that's *any* way close to the same thing.

OK. You're right about that. But I *have* a mother, Norma. I've had a mother all my life. I see and hear motherhood every day; I feel it. I have a very good mother. You ought to pray that everybody in this city could be as good as my mother. She's good, good, not just nice, not fake, not about church – just good. Compared to the rest of us, my mother is a goddamn saint. She's never been mean in her life, her whole life. There've been times I wanted her to, times *any*body would've said, Rosemary, come *on*! Yeah. Norma, my mother is a fucking angel – and nobody even hates her for it. And why not? Because while she's good, she's not self-righteous. No demands, no rules. She's just good, goddamnit.

He takes a long breath. She has a small life. She's too tired to work; she doesn't breathe clearly anymore. She coughs. That job she had, for over thirty years, made her sick. That's what I think. The machines at the back of the cleaners, breathing those chemicals every day in there. She coughs a lot. It's a situation.

So Dwayne, if she doesn't work at the cleaners any more, your mother, what does she do? How does she spend her time these days, this angel? What does your sainted mother do every day of her saintly life? Why *don't* I know her better, anyway? You know my kids, but I don't know your mother. Why not? I'm just realizing you haven't told me much, really.

Not enough, anyway.

Don't be snotty, Norma. It's not useful. This is what she does now: She listens to the radio. She goes to the supermarket and reads *The National Enquirer* and the other rags while she stands in the checkout line, probably coughing a little. She calls me at the shop and talks for maybe two minutes because I tell her I want to hear from her, every day. She walks in the park and sits on the benches and looks at the lake. She talks to my Uncle G because he calls her every day, and she sees him a few times a week. I visit a few times each week, so she can offer me food I don't want. We laugh a little, not too much because she coughs. She sees her friends, but not so much any more. She hasn't done any needlework for over a year. She sleeps a lot and she eats chocolate. She coughs some more, probably from the damn chocolate, but she loves it. She takes medicine before she goes to bed at night. And that's it. That's how Rosemary Clara Larken is going out.

Going out? You make it sound like she's dying, for chrissake.

Dwayne looks away and looks back. His eyes are squinted up.

Wait – are you trying to tell me your mother is dying, Dwayne?

I'm not trying to tell you anything, Norma.

You're saying she's dying? You mean, your mother is dying?

I didn't *mean* to be saying that, no. But ok, yes; she's dying. I ended up saying that because it's true. If you believe the docs over at Illinois Masonic, and I finally do, she's dying from cancer in her lungs, a fifty-two year old woman who never once, not even to see how it tasted, took one drag on a goddamn Lucky Strike. She's dying. She's dying while we're talking about it, Norma, dying all the time now. What she

does now, I should have said when you asked me, is die.
That's mostly what she does, however slowly.

Jesus. Jesus. Dwayne. Dwayne, why didn't you say something?
She strokes his arms, his face, kisses his naked shoulders.
She pulls him down beside her under the quilt, murmuring.
His body is bigger than her children's bodies, but the need in
it, and the impulse that need generates in her, are the same.
She knows how to do this.

In the quiet, Gracie comes back. She sees the fighting is over
and hears the whispered comforting, so she climbs onto the
bed, where the soft voice of her mother soon puts her back
to sleep.

Norma says quietly, conversationally, Here's something I
noticed about Rosemary those two times I did meet her: she
pronounces your name Duh-wayne, but you say Dwayne,
just like that, one syllable. Why's that?

Oh, I'm sure the pronunciation thing is from how long she
lived in Kentucky compared to me. She told me, long time
ago, maybe when we were still there, she chose my name
to rhyme, to match up with, Gawain – my Uncle G's name.
That's his name, and he *is* named after the knight.

Dwayne holds up his hand, raises his eyebrows and shakes
his head once, slowly, to let her know he's not going to
discuss that part of the story; it's a given, a fact.

Everybody back home pronounced it Guh-wain. But she
changed the spelling, she said, so I didn't have to be my
uncle's follow-along. She told me when I was small, this
way I'd have my name and Uncle G'd have his. G doesn't
even use the name. It's on his driver's license and all, but
everybody calls him G, since pretty much always. Norma,
I don't believe I have ever heard anybody, even my mother,
call him Gawain. Not in Chicago, that's for sure.

Naming is a big deal, I think. My sons are named for their father and my father. The first time, I wasn't conscious yet, not yet thinking, so I just accepted the idea of a boy getting his father's name – you know, Junior or "the second." I had not even a glimmer of what Rosemary obviously understood, that everybody should have their own name and not be a small version of somebody else. The second time, I did have a glimmer, but it wasn't enough; I just thought it was good we used a name from my family, instead of Ronny's – I thought that made it *fair*. With Gracie, though, I had begun to be a person.

Norma stroked the little body under the quilt between them. Her name is *her* name. Actually, I got it from Gracie Allen, on tv. I loved her and I loved the relationship between her and George Burns – did you like that show? And I sure got a kick out of the fact that both families approved my choice because they think "Grace" is so Catholic. I did get it right on my last try.

I knew it a little from radio. We didn't have tv at our place; Rosemary still doesn't want it. G always had it, soon as there was money to get it. I offered to get her one, but she's not interested. She likes an occasional movie, especially at one of those big old fancy downtown theaters, but at home, she likes radio. Says she'd rather imagine the story herself, make her own pictures. I know sometimes she sees tv other places – probably with neighbors and friends, or in shops; I believe at the cleaners they put one in the back where the pressers could watch it. But she's never really liked it – especially the commercials. She says, and I'm quoting here, pretty much word for word: You know they are louder, those ads, they are louder than the shows, Dwayne, and that little burst of loud talking always surprises me in a way I don't like. No, I can't say I care for it. I like to sit in the park if I'm going to *watch*. On the radio, ads never seem to surprise me that same way, honey. But maybe I'm just used to it, I don't know.

Now, though, I keep thinking she should have it for later, for the last part, you know, the weeks she'll be mostly in bed. I think then she might change her mind.

Norma kisses his eyelids, which are wet. I can't imagine that, Dwayne. With what you just told me, I can't imagine she'd want tv then any more than she's ever wanted it. But I bet she'd like G, and you – and maybe even me and some other people I don't even know – to talk to her, tell her what we see and hear every day, tell what we're thinking about. Tell her what's in the tabloids, keep her up to date like on those phone calls you two have. Maybe read them to her?

Gracie sits up, slipping the warm quilt off all three of them. I could read to Rosemary! I could do it too! I'm almost done learning how.

One late afternoon in April, when Rosemary no longer calls the shop every day because talking on the phone makes her cough too much, Dwayne walks into Norma's kitchen and says, Hey lady, I can't believe it: we're neither of us working and we're in the same place at the same time. Today was the first slow day that shop has had in months. I shouldn't say this, but I'm happy to have it. When you called, I was already thinking of closing early; I sent Cal and Stevie home. He takes out a mug, fills the kettle, puts it on a burner. He opens the cupboard where Norma keeps tea, and rummages among the jars and boxes.

Dwayne, I called because I need to talk to you. Gracie's over at Sylvie's, so we can talk now.

This is something we can't talk about with Gracie here?

I think so. Probably. Yes, it is. Dwayne, I'm pregnant. Not very pregnant, but definitely pregnant, four or five weeks along. Remember that time the rubber came off inside of me? I'm thinking that's when it happened.

She sits down at the table. He sits down at the table. He looks at her serious face for nearly as long as a minute. Then he says, We're having a baby.

She smiles – sadly, ironically, wistfully, even kindly – and says, No. No, actually, I'm having an abortion.

Dwayne gets up, walks around the kitchen, sits back down and says, What?

Norma says, Listen to me, Dwayne. I've been going over this in my head, over and over it. You know I really care for you. But I have to think about who I am, what my situation is. I have three children, the littlest one living with me. I am able, just now, on my own, to keep that one and me set up with enough macaroni every week while I try, really hard, to be a photographer. That's who I want to be and what I want to do. That's the life you've encouraged, supported, appreciated and appeared to admire for the past six months. You know, like I admire *your* work – your art, your business, the way you run the shop, the way you treat Cal and Stevie, how you're a decent boss *and* a good artist, a man who doesn't have his head up his ass. All of that. All of that's how I thought you thought about me and Gracie and my boys and my camera.

I do think of you that way! You know I think of you that way! Why would having this baby mean I don't think of you that way?

Because if I have this baby I won't be that person anymore. Can't you see? I won't be that way for you to think of. Are you, really, thinking of *me*? I mean, now?

He doesn't say anything. She waits.

I can't see how you could not want to be a mother.

Goddamnit, Dwayne, I *am* a mother. What the hell are you talking about?

Norma, listen. This baby could make up for the boys, replace the boys. No. No, no, I don't mean "replace," I mean – oh, you know what I mean. This could be a good thing, Norma, good for you.

Replace my boys? My boys have not disappeared, Dwayne. They're not missing. They don't live with me, but they have not disappeared. And if – may it never happen – if they *were* to disappear, this baby wouldn't be them. Don't you know that? It'd never be Rontu, never be Jack, never be either one of them. It's somebody else, somebody entirely else. Nobody can replace anybody else. I'd have thought you knew that. Everybody is who they are and no one is replaceable. Ok, in one sense, like if Cal quit, you'd "replace" him – but then it wouldn't be Cal, would it? The new guy? He'd be somebody else; Cal would be gone, not there anymore. Don't you see that? Can't you see that?

Norma's almost shouting by the time she gets to the end of the last sentence.

Dwayne says, I'm going to go, Norma. I'm thinking we're not doing each other any good right now. We can talk about this later.

We can talk about this later or never, Dwayne. I'm taking care of business.

After Dwayne leaves, Norma sits without moving for several minutes. Then she gets up and walks around the apartment, making a little circuit through the rooms, touching pieces of furniture. Then she calls Sylvie and says she's coming over to get Gracie. Before saying goodbye she says, Sylvie, I need to talk to you.

Once there, finding Gracie and Carlos asleep, Norma takes her jacket off and sits down.

Sylvie says, You need to talk to me... about what?

Sylvie, I've got a problem.

Don't we all – oh, sorry – sorry, sorry, sorry! I wasn't looking at your face when you said that. I can see now, from the hairline down; it's a big thing. What's the matter? Tell me.

You know how tired I've been the past few months, doing all these night shoots, taking advantage of you and Dwayne and half a dozen other good people to be with Gracie. Well, Dwayne's been really busy too, and you know his mother is very sick, so he's not exactly got a brain on fire either. But that doesn't mean we haven't had time for sex, every little once in a while.

Uh-oh. Is this story going to endanger my respect for you by revealing you both were so tired you lost the capacity for contraceptive use?

No, but you're close. It was maybe five-six weeks ago; we fucked so late, we fell asleep with him still inside me. At about four in the morning, Gracie called out. I woke right up – of course – but barely conscious, on automatic, you know how it is, that middle-of-the-night fog. When I got her a little cup of water and bent down to kiss her, I realized the rubber was still inside of me because I felt the semen sliding down my thighs. I was so sleepy-stupid I fell back into bed anyway, cleaned myself up in the morning. I told Dwayne – now I wonder what he was thinking – but then I sorta forgot about it. Too much else going on. Then, when it was time to bleed, I didn't. That's it, Sylvie. I can't have this baby. I really can't have this baby. And when I told Dwayne, today, he, it, the conversation... didn't go well. He was... not who I thought he'd be, not who I thought he was, you know?

She cries, partly from embarrassment, partly from relief at saying it all, partly because Sylvie's right: it's a big thing. She cries quietly, to not wake the children.

Norma. Honey. I'm so sorry. So sorry you have to deal with this. She embraces her, reaches over and grabs a box of tissues. She hands it to Norma and waits for her to stop crying. She rubs Norma's back.

In practical terms, aside from everything else – everything else including how this looks like the end for Dwayne and me – I gotta find an abortionist. I don't even know where to start, how to start. How would you do it? You've always been more political than me – more streetwise. How do I *do* this? What do you think?

Sylvie actually smiles. She says, What *I* think is, you're going to have to treat me to a really good dinner, maybe ribs at that near-North place with the fantastic sauce – because I have a number you can call. It's a group of women who help other women in Chicago have abortions.

Sylvie! Ohmigod, Sylvie! Norma bursts into tears again, this time so loudly that Sylvie pulls half the tissues out of the box in a lump and presses them onto Norma's face, to stifle the noise so Carlos and Gracie don't wake up.

How did you get that number? Have you… did you have… wouldn't you have told me… if you had an abortion?

I haven't had one, but I know these women. I trust them. I know you can trust them. I did some work with them a couple times, helping out a little. I know women who've gone to them, to their underground clinic.

Norma sits up straight, sniffles, blows her nose – quietly – a few times. She says, Sylvie, this is a moment that screams for my favorite cliché: *I can never thank you enough.*

For the first time since high school, Norma remembers jokes about St Scholastica being conveniently located near The Cradle, the big Evanston adoption agency. She tells Sylvie about her cousin from the suburbs who got pregnant and was sent down to St Louis, to a home for unwed mothers. And – ohmigod, she hasn't thought of this for years – Ronny's sister Jeanne, that bitch who's giving her such a hard time these days, suddenly, *out of nowhere,* took junior year abroad when everybody knew her parents were against that whole program. The Sheridans consider all of Europe except the Vatican a bad influence.

She remembers the rumors and jokes she didn't understand then: about sex and babies, about "getting caught," stories about girls in trouble, being careful, keeping your legs together. These things all come burbling out of Norma as she sniffles and blows her nose. One of the stories, maybe the one about her sister-in-law, sparks a laughing fit. Tissues depleted, Sylvie hands her a sofa pillow to press over her face, and waits it out.

They talk a long time, grateful for the deep baby sleep of their children. To Sylvie's questions, Norma insists that yes, she does, definitely absolutely positively with no doubt about it intend to have an abortion – and there really isn't anything powerful enough to argue against what she knows to be her own reality, her own necessity.

I've had it with following the old rules, Sylvie; they don't work for me. The models we grew up with don't fit – you know what I mean. We just have to figure out how we're supposed to live. When I left Ronny, I thought I'd have my tubes tied. Then I thought, why bother, it's not like I'm fucking anybody. And I didn't have the money anyway. Then, when I started having sex with Dwayne, I figured, ok, turns out there is one man I want to fuck, there may be others, I better deal with it – but I still didn't have the money. Needless to say, working as a free-lancer, there's no insurance – and my guess is it wouldn't be covered anyway.

You know I took the pill 'til I understood how unhealthy it was; I had an IUD that gave me a miscarriage; I think diaphragms are messier than rubbers. So there you are. I mean, there *I* am. I am scrupulous, not to say compulsive, about using rubbers – I keep 'em in my bag and have a stash in the drawer by my bed. I guess what I'm saying here is I've been good. Not that it saved me. But given that you trust these women, these secret underground women, shouldn't you be cheering for me? I mean, why do you keep asking these questions?

I want you to be sure, Norma. Not just because you're my friend, either. One thing I've learned from these abortion service women – they're called Janes – is these decisions are complicated; they're *always* complicated. Look, if you had lots of money, I mean *lots* of money, like Ethel Kennedy, so you didn't have to work for pay, would you consider having this baby then? I bet Dwayne would be a good father. He's rare – a man who actually loves his mother as the person she is? Jeez Louise.

Sylvie! Leave Dwayne out of the conversation. Please. It's too embarrassing to think how I was wrong about Dwayne. The way he responded! I can't believe I was so wrong about him. I don't want to talk about him anymore. Maybe not ever, but for sure not now.

Ok, no Dwayne. No talking about Dwayne. Here's where I'm coming from with the questions: this service is set up to help women who decide to have abortions. Hundreds of women and girls call them. Hundreds, every week, all the time! So the Janes have to be sure those women are sure, you know? And hey, in the realm of being sure, I think you should get a pregnancy test.

Oh, come on. You think I don't know my own body? I've got three kids and a cycle so regular you can check it against the goddamn moon.

You should do it, Norma – you never *really* know unless you really *know*.

Is that like extra innings at Wrigley Field: It ain't over 'til it's over?

Yeah – it *is* like that. Exactly like that. If you're worried about getting in to see your regular doc, or what he'll say – no, wait, isn't he your uncle? Forget him. There's some women on the south side doing pregnancy tests – you pay a small donation to cover costs, or get it free if you need to, like with the Janes; I'll give you their number. For the abortion, the Service charges a hundred dollars or whatever you can afford. I'll get you set up with a Jane for counseling – unless you call me with good news after that test.

I can't believe this! My friend Sylvie is a woman who knows abortionists – *and* women who do pregnancy tests – all these feminist renegades! … Um, Syl, please don't think I'm chickenshit, but, will you be there when I do it? Will you come with me? I don't want to go alone. Don't think I don't believe you, I'm sure you're right, I'm sure they're good women. But I don't want to go alone.

Of course! Maybe when everything's so cool we've got a big national monument to all the women and girls who've ever had abortions, *then* everybody could go alone if they want. Check in with me as soon as they give you an appointment time. We'll get somebody to stay with Carlos and Gracie that day.

When Dwayne left Norma's apartment, he went down to the street, got into his car and sat there for a while. For several minutes he didn't think. Nothing happened inside his mind, and his body was still. Then a horn honked close by, and he jerked his head. A car was idling in the lane beside his parking space, its driver gesturing and mouthing the words, Are you pulling out?

Dwayne nodded, aware of both irony and contradiction. He said – out loud, softly, to himself – No. It's too late.

He headed for the lake. When he got to the Drive he turned south, to G's place. He was going to let himself in with his key and wait, but that turned out not to be necessary. He took it as a sign; G being home makes him think this is a conversation he's supposed to have.

Dwayne says he has something to talk about and then repeats, pretty much word for word, the first three or four sentences of the conversation he had with Norma. He does it fairly – that is, with no editing or commentary.

His uncle says, Ah. Ah. Yeah, that is something to talk about, all right. Want a beer?

Dwayne nods.

G hands him a bottle of Dos Equis from the fridge.

That's rough, Dwayne. That's a rough situation. I'm sorry to hear it, boy; you got my sympathy. Is this your first time? First of any or first with a woman you care for?

First and only, I hope. This is not something I'd want to do repeatedly.

Well, nobody does it on purpose, Dwayne boy. Me, for instance – I'm careful enough to keep my cock in a Brinks truck, but you better believe I've had to deal with this. Thing is, Dwayne, there's nothing foolproof, and you don't have to be a fool to get caught. The science boys, they can put guys on the moon but they don't seem to be able to help us out here. You gotta wonder, right?

Yeah, sure, but it's not just them. Human error isn't going away, G. That's pretty much how it was with Norma and me; we use rubbers – good ones, no gas station Brand X – but we fell asleep together, combined in that good way. You know how that feels like a good thing. But this time it wasn't.

All's I mean to say here is, this is a no-blame situation. You're not in the wrong, and she's not blaming you, right? 'Cept for wanting her to have it, I mean. So let's look at that – what's that about? I mean, what's that for, Dwayne? Fatherhood – have you gotten interested in that? You never did want that before. I tell you why I put it that way, boy. When you say you want Norma to have this baby, I think, hmmm – what for? How'd Dwayne come to feel that way, after all this time? At this exact moment. What moment is this, what else is going on in this moment? … You see where I'm headed here? What comes to mind, to my mind, is your mama. I think, maybe, what you want is for Norma to – maybe, I'm just saying maybe on this – start up a replacement. He puts up his hand – a stop sign.

Now Dwayne, I feel like I can say this to you because we're together in this here moment in time I'm talking about. Because your mama is leaving us both, and we gotta think about it. We gotta think about it in some serious ways, and now is not too soon. She has been right in the middle of both our lives for a whole long time, and soon enough that won't be the truth anymore.

Dwayne sits, beer bottle in hand. When the cold bottle has chilled his fingers enough to sting, he says, That's some notion, G. Not about mama dying – no argument there. I know it's coming, and I know it won't be long. She could go before winter. But the idea of expecting Norma to make me a replacement – a new somebody to love. That doesn't speak very well of me, does it? Wait – it's still my turn. Don't start talking 'til I stop; I'm just taking a breather here… Ok. Now. That replacement thing is a recurrent theme, Uncle G. I really fried Norma's circuits using that word, and I'm thinking you're about to fry mine.

You *told* her you wanted a baby to replace your mother? What'd Norma say? I imagine she might not think that was a good reason for her to make a person. I mean, on top of how she has got a bunch of kids already.

No, no, no. That's not how it went. I said, sort of – I definitely fumbled this – that maybe she could think of this new baby as a replacement for the boys – her sons, that were given up to their father's custody by the court.

Dwayne boy, you're lucky to have gotten out of there alive. Saying that to a mother! I'll tell you, here's what happened to you, son. You got caught in the vainlight. It's like that deer-in-the-headlights thing, only it's internal. Vainlight's how we all see pretty much most of the time: everybody sees mostly their own self. In some people that light is so bright they can't see nothing *but* their own selves, ever. Thing is, it's ironic: they can't see themselves clearly, see how they really are, because their vainlight is so bright it blinds them. You're not that kind, Dwayne, nothing like. But this time, well, your vainlight flared up, because you're in a dire situation. You knowing Rosemary's dying, thinking about what that means, even when you're not – you know, even when it's unconscious – and here comes Norma with this news. You gotta think – even if you don't know you're thinking it – this could be a baby Ro. That's what comes to mind here. That's what comes to my mind, knowing you like I do, since you were born.

What came to Dwayne's mind was that he wanted to talk to Rosemary. He wanted to talk to her even knowing it could make her cough, even believing it'd make her unhappy. This odd choice, this not-like-Dwayne impulse got stronger when he left G's place. It ran across the bottom of his mind where he could see it, like a translation at the movies: I'll talk to Mama about this. He set it aside as he drove north up Halsted, going back home the slowest way. He set it aside when he got in bed, switched off the lamp and rolled over, jamming the pillow between his ear and shoulder.

But it came back; the impulse did not leave him. A few days later, swishing the dregs of his morning drink around in the blender jar, he decided to do it. He looked out the window; the bus was coming and the people waiting at the corner moved closer to the curb. Sick as she is, he's going to do it. He wants her to talk to him the way she did when she was his guide, years he was not yet responsible for his whole life.

When he's sitting in her kitchen, she does talk to him that way.

Mama, you know it's against the law, don't you? This operation Norma wants to sign up for, it's illegal. Abortion is against the law.

Oh yes, honey, has been all my life, most everwhere. But you know, Dwayne, law's not everthing. Lots of people do things against the law, some of 'em good people too. I believe *you* have used what're called "illegal substances." She closes her eyes. Don't tell me about it one way or the other. And I believe you work on soldier boys too young by state law. You give 'em the pictures they want; I know you do, Dwayne.

She touches his anxious face.

Back home, the midwife who helped me with you, she was against the law, no gold-trimmed paper framed up on the wall in her cabin. But she caught you, and had done me, and your Uncle G too. And she'd done abortions, Sister Honna, of course she did; she did all the necessary work for women.

Oh she was good at it, all of it, but she was against the law. I wish she was up here now, Dwayne; I'm thinkin there won't be a woman like that up here to take care of your Norma. To help you both. Where will she go, Dwayne? Honey, you got to be thinkin about this in some different ways. The ways you're thinkin now, they're not what you need. They're what you think you need, but I can't see that need lasting. I believe I know who you are.

This speech leaves Rosemary breathless and coughing, small dry coughs, the hard kind. Dwayne makes chamomile tea, puts it on the table with honey and a spoon, sits down beside her with a cup of his own.

You came here because you want me to tell you what all I think, and I am. I'm telling you.

They drink their tea. Then Rosemary starts to talk again; her voice is rough, but clear.

Here's one of these different ways to think, Dwayne. Do you imagine it could be good for a baby, coming to a mama doesn't want it? You know I wanted you – and I wanted more, too. But what if I didn't, I mean, if I didn't want you back then? I can't hardly stand to think of how that would have been! How bad it'd be, terrible bad, to have a little bitty thing growing, turning into a person inside you and you unhappy, worried, scared. The mama knowing she won't love it, can't feed it. Oh Dwayne, what if those tiny babies know too, when they get big enough to have feelings, time they're ready to come out; what if they know their mama doesn't want them?

She pauses to cough. She sips the tea and coughs more but easier, not dry.

Honey, I believe you care for Norma, and Gracie too. Gracie! Oh, my goodness, Dwayne, what'd that be like for our little friend Gracie? And those boys! Their mama unhappy all the time, and a new baby unhappy too? Have you been thinking about that, son? About how Norma's already got three children? Even with those boys being stolen away from her, even with just those few days ever month she sees her boys, they are her boys, like you're mine.

Dwayne suddenly wonders if Norma has called Rosemary and told her what he said that night.

He helps his mother walk from the kitchen to the sofa – she says she doesn't want to go to sleep – and he goes out, telling Rosemary he wants to re-fill her prescription before the drug store closes.

Downstairs in the doorway, Dwayne stands still. As he had been in the car outside Norma's apartment, he is mindless and unmoving. If he's thinking, it's like a dream; his mind is doing it without him, outside of his knowing. He does go to the drug store, but at the counter, reaching into his pocket, he realizes he's not brought the prescription. To the pharmacist, who's looking at him with what might be sympathetic interest, he says, Oh. I didn't bring the prescription. I'll come back tomorrow. Sorry. Thanks. Sorry. Sorry to bother you.

Then he walks back to his mother's apartment. He walks faster and his mind clears; it wakes up. He's got one more thing to say. Rosemary greets him when he opens the door and he smiles to find her awake. Dwayne sits down next to her on the sofa, takes one of her hands in both of his and says the one more thing he's thought of to say.

Mama, if this baby is a boy, I'd want to name him Clovis.

Rosemary smiles and says, I know you mean that for a good thing, Dwayne. But son, I'd only see that baby for a tiny while – a tiny while can't be made as big as Norma's life, or, oh my heaven, a new little one's life. You know it'd be just a bit of time. Of course you do. I know you do. I'll be gone. Norma and Gracie and those boys and that baby will be here. You think that baby'd make me happy. But you know what? How happy could I be, knowing Norma's not happy at all?

Norma was not happy at all when he called, saying he wanted to give her money, asking how much she needed, to pay for it.

You can't even say the word, can you? I don't want money from you, Dwayne. And you shouldn't buy something you don't want. *I* want this abortion; it's for me, not you. I'll pay for it.

Norma, don't be silly. You don't have the money, and I do.

Thank you for that reminder of one more important difference between us, Mr. Larken. I think we've come to a good place to end this conversation.

She hangs up, and when she does, the phone rings again. It's not Dwayne. It's a woman who says, Hello. This is Jane. Is this Norma? Sylvie gave me your number.

When her abortion's over, Norma's tired. She says, Sylvie, I feel like I just walked from the Museum of Science and Industry to Belmont Harbor – carrying all my camera equipment. How many miles is that?

When they pick up the children at playgroup, they agree Sylvie will keep Gracie overnight – in case of anything; she tells Norma to call later, to check in. Norma opens the door to the backseat and leans in to say goodbye with kisses. Gracie-love, have a good time – I'll see you later; bye-bye Carlos.

Then she sticks her head in the front window. Sylvie. Sylvie Sylvie Sylvie – it goes without saying, but I'm gonna say it anyway: *Any*time you need *any*thing, I'm the one you call: no question, no hesitation. She blows a kiss to the car as they pull away.

She feels good the next morning, wakes up early in spring sunshine with no memory. Then she moves and feels the thick sanitary napkin against her vulva; it's a feeling she hasn't had since her second year of high school. Instantly Norma recalls the day she and Lucia Martinotti locked themselves in the bathroom to insert their first tampons – even though their mothers had warned them that would mean they weren't virgins anymore.

This sanitary napkin is one of three given her by the Jane who sat beside the bed, held her hand and talked to her during the abortion. When Norma left, that Jane told her, Nothing – and I mean *nothing* – goes inside for the first month.

This day, the day after, Norma does a real estate shoot and takes Gracie to the park right from playgroup. It's light out long enough to make a difference, but they both fall asleep by eight o'clock. It's late afternoon on the next day when she sees a newspaper and reads about the bust. Taking a break between gigs, she's at The Gold Cup on Clark, where she and Dwayne went for breakfast after the first time they had sex. She's got the paper propped up against the little hot water pot while she drinks her tea.

The abortion service was raided the day after her appointment. Seven Janes were taken to jail and booked on multiple felony homicide charges. Their names and addresses are printed in the article; one is Betsy, the Jane who called her. One is Denah, the writer who got a dolphin on her shoulder at Dwayne's place; there's a picture of her on the front page of the *Daily News*, next to a paragraph saying she's a nursing mother, calling her Mrs. Something. All seven are out on bail.

Jesus H. Christ! Norma thinks so many things so fast she's not even sure she's thinking. Her brain is generating a rapid montage, images and ideas are zipping around, passing the usual comprehension stations, the places they go to get sorted out and classified by whatever parts of her mind usually do that.

Amazingly though, Norma doesn't think of herself, never once worries about her name appearing in impounded records, never wonders if she'll be discovered to have broken the law – if she will appear in the paper like these women, if Ronny will now take Gracie away and never let her see the boys again either. Instead, stuck like a rough splinter in her brain, right where you'd think those fears would be, is a question; she's wondering, did Dwayne do this? Did Dwayne call the cops? Did he report the Service, terrifying two hundred women waiting for abortions this week, endangering every Jane and closing their underground clinic?

She can ask this question; she can imagine Dwayne' making that call.

Norma's rigid with her suspicion. She's looking at the other people in the restaurant – the woman at the cash register, the guy sweeping up. They don't know she's having an extraordinary experience with her newspaper. She reads the article again; there's no mention of how the police knew, how they got the address. The front page headline says, Seven Women Arrested in Abortion Ring.

By the next day Norma is having, she thinks, some sort of low-level schizophrenic episode. She knows, she believes, knows she believes, that Dwayne had no idea where she was going for her abortion, who was doing it, or even when it was. How could he? Her suspicion, the inside-her-own-head accusation she's making a dozen times a day, is irrational. She can't help thinking it though, can't make it go away. She has created a picture of him picking up the phone to call the police, and it comes to her mind without being sent for; she can't, even when she wants to, make it stay away. It comes back.

After a few more days of this, she calls Betsy. Assuming Jane phones will be tapped, she says, Hey Betsy, it's Norma. I'll be in your neighborhood tomorrow; will you be around?

They go for a walk. Betsy tells her what she knows, what she's heard. One of the women with an appointment that day, May 3rd, told her sister-in-law where she was going, the address of the front, an apartment like the one where Sylvie waited for Norma the day before. That sister-in-law is the one who called the cops. That sister-in-law says Jesus doesn't want women to have abortions.

Myself, Betsy says, just me, I think the woman – the one who was coming to us – wasn't sure. I think maybe she wanted to be stopped, or wanted both things at once, you know? I mean, why tell someone like that? Why choose *her* to meet at the front? Some Janes think people who want to keep abortion illegal put the sister-in-law up to it – they're pretty frantic these days, with possible changes in the law coming down soon. But really, once you move back from action to motive, who can say? We know who she is, and we know she made the call. We may never know why she did it, or why the woman with the appointment even told her.

Norma calls Dwayne that night. She's on a mission.

Dwayne, it's Norma. She doesn't wait for a reply, which is just as well, since he's too surprised to hear from her to say anything. She rushes on. You wanted to give me money. Give it to the Abortion Seven Defense Fund. Write a check for as much as you can to the Abortion Seven Defense Fund.

Now he can talk. You mean those women in the papers? You know them? Have you done it? Did you do it with them? Were you there when they got busted? They say on the news those women have no medical training, Norma. Are you all right? Are you ok? Jesus, Norma. Tell me something.

Yes, I do mean those women in the papers. Yes, I know some of them, now. Yes, it's done, and I did it with them; I was there the day before the bust. They don't have framed diplomas on the walls – they don't have walls, actually, they use their friends' apartments, but they do have the skills they need; they're well trained. Do you think I'm a fool, Dwayne?

This time Dwayne wonders if Rosemary has called and told Norma about Sister Honna in Kentucky.

Write the check, Dwayne. At least a hundred. Their price is a hundred or whatever the woman can afford. If you'd paid for me, it would have been a hundred.

Dwayne says nothing. She waits. Then he says, Ok, I'll do this. Should I bring it over? I'd like to see you, Norma, talk to you.

This isn't about us, Dwayne. Somebody will come and get it at the shop. She hangs up.

A few days later, Sylvie walks into Dwayne's place. Dwayne is working, but he sees her and nods. I'm about done here, Sylvie; can you wait?

She goes over to the couch and picks up, deliberately, slowly, a copy of *Sports Illustrated* – to irritate the guys, Dwayne thinks. In about ten minutes he's done with a red heart that says *Always and Ever*; when the guy is gone, he turns to Sylvie.

Are you here for some art, or are you the messenger I've been told to expect?

She laughs. I'm here on assignment, Dwayne.

He sighs. He reaches into the cabinet next to his chair and hands her an envelope. Here it is. But can I ask you a couple questions? Cal and Stevie exchange a look, which Dwayne sees. Let's go across the street; I'll buy you a cup of coffee.

They sit down in a booth at Dooley's and he says, Sylvie, what are my chances? I probably should say, do I *get* any chances? What do you think is going to happen between me and Norma? Should I try to make contact, should I hang on, or should I just start getting over it?

Dwayne, you know I can't be absolutely positive – but I think maybe if you can figure out what to do, what to say, you might get a chance to do it and say it.

He smiles as if his mouth is tired.

I know before this thing, this crisis, Norma really cared for you, cared about you. She does think about you now – though *what* she thinks is the hard part. Even so, she always talked about you, about the shop, about your guys. And your mother – she's pretty sick, right? How's she doing? I know Norma was worried.

Ah, let's not mix up too many hard things, Sylvie. My mama's going down. She's going down. How's Gracie?

Oh, she's fine. She and Carlos play tattoo – she's you; I'd say her flash is mostly cubist. Anyway – thing is, what I can tell you about Norma is, in relation to you, she's crazed. I don't know what you said that day, but it pretty much cut right through her brain. We talk freely, Norma and me, but she hasn't told me that. I'm assuming it's too hard, it'd cost her too much, to say the words.

He starts to speak and she says, I'm not asking you to tell me. That's the truth; I'm really not. I'm just trying to give you a sense of how it is with her. You asked me and I'm telling you. You must have stuck a knife in the worst possible place, 'cause it cut real bad. But here's the thing, Dwayne, like my uncle Teddy always says, Wounded ain't crippled and sick ain't dead. My opinion is, it's too soon to know. Since this hasn't made you leave town by now, why not stick around a while longer? Sounds like you're not looking for a replacement right away – Dwayne actually laughs at this, an ugly laugh – so why not wait and see? I think she's working on finding a way out of this, maybe working on finding a way back to you. That's just a guess, of course.

He smiles that tired smile again, moving his lips like he's just been to the dentist.

Sylvie holds up the envelope and thanks him for it. She leans across the booth and pins a metal button to his shirt. It's dark blue and says in white letters: Free the Abortion Seven. There's your receipt.

In the middle of June, Cal answers the phone at the shop: Tattoo. What? Yeah. Yes. He's right here. Dwayne, phone.

This is Dwayne.

Hey Dwayne, I've just gotten back from the market, says Norma. I'm new to this business, so I only got some M&M's. I did separate the colors right away, though, before I called.

Dwayne doesn't say anything for several seconds. He stands still. Then he says, Ah. And then he says, Are there even amounts?

No way. Never. I bet if that ever happened, and you called the company, they'd have to give you a prize. No, as usual, there are more dark Browns than anything, the double chocolates. Reds are in second place. I did get three Greens, though.

Ah.

I wish you could use the register at the manager's station when you're only buying stuff as small as this. I told him. I said I was sure his customers would like that. His answer, you will not be surprised to hear, was like a recorded message.

He said, "Thank you for that suggestion. We appreciate our customers taking an interest in the market." He sounded just like a robot – if you closed your eyes you could maybe imagine him looking like the one in the movie where Michael Rennie is Klaatu, where the robot looks like the Tin Man's big brother? I can't remember the robot's name. You know, I bet; what's it called, Dwayne?

Gort. It's Gort.

Yes! Yes! Norma doesn't say anything for several seconds. Well, truth is, it didn't really take me so long to buy those M&Ms. I didn't have a chance to read anything. I'll catch some news for you next time, though. Bye, Dwayne.

Bye, Norma. See you later.

Men of God in the 21ˢᵗ Century

A motley group of clergymen began meeting less than a year after the Roberts court overturned the Roe v. Wade decision of their 1973 predecessors. Here's a partial transcript taken from FBI files:

John Smith: Truth is, I'm not good at knowing what to say when a woman comes into my office, bursts into tears, tells me she's pregnant and can't have the baby. I think probably I need to have a woman in there with me, talking.

Sam Abramowitz: Can you have someone from the congregation join you for those meetings?

John Smith: Thing is, I don't always know, when she says she wants to talk to me, *that*'ll be the subject of the conversation – I don't have anybody on call or nearby I can get to right away, when the conversation goes that way.

Ahmed Mustafah: Whoa, wait a minute here. I don't think it's a good idea to bring members of your congregation into what might turn out to be criminal activity.

Joe Cohen: I agree with Ahmed; what we need is some kind of training, so we can be better at talking with these women.

Doug Grayson: Do we need to do more than give referrals?

Stan McKellen: Yes! Don't you guys consider this a part of pastoral counseling? I mean, these women are coming to us with a serious emotional problem, something that requires guidance and comfort, the same way they'd come to us for anything else, like if they found out their kids were using drugs or their partners unfaithful – whatever. Even though abortion is illegal again, the counseling part is the same as it always was. Think about what that guy in Wichita had to go through – probably *still* has to deal with even now – having George Tiller assassinated right there in his church! What would *that* feel like? PTSD for the whole congregation, right? Tiller was a deacon, for Lord's sake! Hey, don't look at me like that, you guys. I can't help thinking about these things.

Sam Abramowitz: I hear he's had a lot of community support, and some seminary students as back-up. You know, we only hear about the yahoos, but there are some good people out there in Wichita. Anyway, in terms of your question, yeah, that's what I think – but really, we need to deal with a bunch of different elements here, which is why I still say we ought to talk to some of the old guys, the ones who were doing hard stuff in the early civil rights movement in the fifties and sixties, and the ones who did *this* before Roe. Some of them are still alive – and some are still active.

Charlie Washington: Right. And guys, don't forget lots of us have been working in opposition to secular law in other ways – some of us went public, talked to the media about gay marriage and commitment ceremonies, about "illegal" immigrants taking sanctuary in the church. Like other times in history, including the clergy who defied slavery – or Hitler.

Ahmed Mustafah: Yeah, all six of 'em.

Joe Cohen: Hey! Good one – you're one more funny Semite, Ahmed. Ok, the most absolutely basic thing we need to know is, where's it safe to send these women? We just can't ever forget what we're doing is against the law now. It's like draft counseling was, or helping members of the Guard and the Army get out – isn't it?

Bob Sanders: Ok, so, yes, we have to train ourselves, train each other, to actually be of comfort, to be supportive in the face of all the related issues, and to show them how making an abortion decision is actually within their religious tradition, is historically –

Ahmed Mustafah: *I'm* worried about how we deal with the more conservative (to say the least) of our *colleagues* – we need to talk about how that's going to work. In my case, and you guys all know this, those people are after me all the time, and they raid my congregation, for young men especially –

Doug Grayson: You know, that's starting to happen to me, too – the hellfire guys, one in particular, are openly critical of me. They put on a show every Sunday – and you know about those bozos on tv! I'm too reasonable, my wife says, too "low-key." And I'm thinking, well, what am I supposed to do?

Charlie Washington: Don't laugh, brothers, but I'm using hip-hop; I'm doing a rap sermon at one of my Sunday services, and the place rocks. Most of the parents and grandparents are grateful. You know me – I prefer gospel, I'm an oldtime-religion kind of guy, but I want those kids and they want that stuff, so I'm *on it*. Hey, I got me a dj for the Sunday school – why not?

Sam Abramowitz: Hey yourself; I'm not laughing, Charlie. I've got a hot klezmer group coming to my shul every other Friday to play at the Oneg Shabbat and alternate weeks at the Sunday School; one of the musicians does stand-up. Just like you, I want the kids. I want them *laughing*!

Jefferson Darnley: At the meeting house, we've got a film series the kids like; right after Roverturn we focused on pregnancy choices with a double feature – *Dirty Dancing* and *Juno*. It was a big success; they couldn't stop talking. So we're going to do it again, with *Spitfire Grill* and *Ciderhouse Rules*, or maybe *Obvious Child*.

Charlie Washington: Yep, that's right – pay attention to what they enjoy, and then you know what to do next. Like, when even guys with gang tattoos show up, I know I'm heading in the right direction.

John Smith: What happened with that guy in Michigan – pastor called Benting or Bentley or something? The one who opened a tattoo parlor in his church a couple years ago? Did that stick? More important, did it *work*?

Bob Sanders: I don't know, but when I read about him doing it, I loved that the set-up was right by the baptism tank. I thought right away, when I read that, this guy is *bold*! But, anyway, I want to change the subject – I need to bring up something that's been bothering me about our group here: we're still men only – I mean, I know in the sixties that was a fact of life for the Concerned Clergy network, but why don't the women clergy come to our meetings now? What's that *about*? What're we doing wrong?

Doug Grayson: I think they're meeting with nurse-midwives and other women doing healthcare; I think their primary identity around these issues is the woman thing, not the clergy thing. I could be off base here, but that's what it looks like to me.

Ahmed Mustafah: I definitely need help with this, guys; I've got serious gender issues at my mosque – gender *and* generation gaps, getting wider all the time.

Stan McKellen: Ok. I'm going to call a couple women I know – one's a Methodist, one's Presbyterian. I wish we had some radical Episcopalians! Not one Episcopal priest comes to these meetings – even though, in some sense, they're "more radical than thou" – than me, anyway. They've got social justice history in this country. But yeah – it's weird to have us gay male clergy here but nobody from the girls' team. More alliances! We need more alliances. Coalition! Networking! And [*a chorus of voices joins him*] Outreach! Underground outreach – a contradiction in terms!

Jefferson Darnley: What about Mormons? Do any of you know those guys? Are they still impenetrable, or corrupt like Scientologists? How about that radical priest at St Simone? We've never, correct me if I'm wrong here, had a Catholic priest come to our meetings. But *that guy*, the one old Sweeney ranted about in Chicago – probably that's what finally killed Sweeney, undead for as long as he was – you know, the one in the feature story in the *NY Times Magazine*? Whether the Pope likes him or not, *I* sure do.

Bob Sanders: Somehow I doubt the opinion of a Quaker is going to carry much weight in that situation.

John Smith: Are you guys out of your minds? Why are you even talking about this? I mean, why not a vampire pastor? A zombie minister? They'd be about as likely – and more popular with the kids, too.

Charlie Washington: No, no, John! You're not paying enough attention to the progressive wing of the RCC. You gotta start reading *Conscience*. Those people *rock*.

Ahmed Mustafah: Oh, thanks guys – thank you all. That'll help a lot at my place; that's just what I need out in front, a pack of infidels with priests' collars.

Joe Cohen: Well Ahmed, since we're all into breaking the law for God, there won't be much going on "out in front," so I don't think you have to worry about that. Not right now, anyway. Not yet.

Denah & the Strawberry, Talking

Denah says, Are you telling me you want a name? I mean, a real name? Is it not ok for me to be calling you the Strawberry? Too cute? I suppose you know I'd have named you Franny, after my mother. If I'd kept you, I mean; if you'd been born.

The Strawberry says, Franny's a good name and I like it, but – please don't be offended, Denah, I know how you feel about her – I don't think it's right for me. I always thought her dying young was part of why you're so thoughtful, so careful, about motherhood. I've even wondered if, any of the times you got tattooed, you ever thought about those hearts that say MOTHER. But you know what? I think you're on to something here. You know how sometimes it takes somebody else saying what you think to make you know that's what you think? I *am* interested in having a name.

I used to think those heart tattoos are like Mother's Day cards – mostly phony and superficial. But they *are* classic flash, and I might find the nostalgia appealing; I mean, if I were to do it now. I'm sure some of the people who get them are sincere. I *could* get a heart that says "Franny," or a ribbon with her name on it. There's this woman here in town whose work I really like; she'd do a good job.

Think about it, turn it over in your mind. But right now, let's concentrate on a name for me. I think maybe I need kind of a *trans* name, Denah. Because my gender wasn't done yet when you aborted me. I was, what, 5-6 weeks at most? Practically still an embryo. You can say I'm female, because at that stage every fetus is – but I think I should have a name that's not gender-specific.

I never thought of that! You know, I already had Joey and I'd have wanted a girl if I was going to have another one. I wasn't thinking of *you*, I mean *you* as I know you now – now since this whole relationship, the Strawberry thing, got started. It never occurred to me. Maybe I'm not so thoughtful and careful as you say.

No way. You're a really good mother – to Joey. Our relationship hasn't been much like that. I mean, I've never needed you to *mother* me; we're more like friends than mother-and-child, don't you think? Our relationship is a hybrid anyway, not one or the other. Not ordinary, for sure. In fact, it's a trans thing, another trans thing! Which brings us back to my name; I think you're right. But this is *complicated*.

I'll say! Well, nothing is ever simple, really. That's why making decisions is so tough. That's why those bozos who go around saying "you're either with us or against us," are so dangerous – to say nothing of stupid. Wait, no – they're not all stupid – not actually stupid *per se*. Maybe they think making choices seem easy will encourage people to act. But I doubt it. They just want to simplify reality. I can understand the impulse; don't get me wrong. Being mature and competent is difficult – and it takes time. But I'd rather work at being mature and competent than skip over the reality part, you know?

That's some speech, Denah – especially for a woman who's talking to her aborted fetus, thirty years on. The part about reality? You're cute when you're philosophical, verging on rhetorical. You should write about us, or make a movie! A short one maybe, a cartoon – the abortion could be great in animation! Put that in your notes for when you finish your other one, ok? Now though, what about my name? Let's get back to practical concerns: practicality R us, ok?

Now, don't *you* get offended, but – sometimes I think you're not real, you know? I think I made you up. That we're not really having a two-way conversation here, that you're a projection, a fantasy I made up to help me think about things – like when I talk out loud to people I love who are dead. We've discussed that, haven't we? About how some of the people in my life are dead, some are alive, and I relate to all of 'em? And even though you're not actually a person, never got far enough along to be one, I include you in that. Other times, though, I'm totally positive you're real. And you know, now that we're talking about it, I'd rather have you be real; I think *real* means you're independent.

Independent is good. Let's say I'm real. Yeah, I'd rather be real. Hey, do you think the fact we agree about so much, so many things, is an argument for the influence of genetics? In the nature/nurture argument? No, wait – since we've been doing this for so many years, you could make the case it's learned, environmental. Oh, whatever.

Yeah, and the fact that I have this relationship with you is part of my whole take on the politics of reproductive justice. These conversations with you have influenced me a lot. Like with that piece in the *New York Times Magazine* some years back? You were *so* helpful then! Have you thought any more about those fundamentalist types I told you about? The ones who put all the heaven and god stuff onto their aborted fetuses? I mean, hey, ok, they want to talk to an aborted fetus? Fine, do it – *I* do it. Just don't do it like *that*. Let's have some respect here! I don't even talk to children like *that*, like words are fuzzy booties. I didn't talk like that when Joey was a baby, that fake voice, high-pitched and constantly excited – how so many people talk to babies? And dogs! Lots of 'em even talk to *dogs* that way!

Calm down, Denah. I'm with you on this – all the way.

You know, I used to think about Ethel Kennedy – she had all those kids and seemed to have a really good time with them. Now I think about Angelina Jolie – same thing, except she doesn't make them all herself. I suppose *seemed* is the operative word here – I mean, how the hell do I know what those women think and feel? My point is, the money. If I'd had unlimited money, like those women, would I have wanted unlimited children? That was long before I knew about the outrageous carbon footprint of the USA's consumer-citizens, so, back then, would I have wanted a couple kids? A few? Several? Because, I've said to myself in that mood, with lotsa money I'd have enough time to write *and* raise kids; I wouldn't have to work for pay. Oh, wait – I bet Ethel and Angelina have servants – that doesn't appeal to me, the servant thing. What I've wondered is, if I'd had money, lots of money, pots of money, would I have had you – you think?

No way we can know. Since you ask, I'll say this: Given your work and the things you love, I don't see making more people as an especially good choice. And there was David to consider. It was sweet how he sat on the bed and held your hand when Claudia took me out – a righteous lover, a responsible guy. But he wasn't into being a father, never did want kids, right? Didn't he get a vasectomy after me? So you'd have had all that to deal with if you'd gone that way. Right? Anyway, we're getting way off the subject – my name. Let's concentrate here. What about Leslie, like Leslie Feinberg? She was a trans hero and even her nickname goes both ways. Or, what if I go in another direction – irony. Then maybe Marion, like John Wayne was before Hollywood? Irony ought to figure in this somehow, don't you think?

You should be the one to choose. Finding a name is always hard. It took Eli and me a long time to name Joey. We didn't decide until he was maybe two weeks old. We called him Baby and Honey and Little Bub until we finally got it. And the hospital people were so nasty about it! Like it's their goddamn business anyway. It's all about the paperwork, the birth certificate – but they acted like it'd be bad for the baby not to have a name immediately – they tried to shame us, like we were bad parents. They really pissed me off.

Setting aside the habitual bad behavior of the medical industry, I have to point out that my situation is notably different. From his, I mean. And the other one – the miscarriage? Talk about "notably different"! We'll *never* know who that was.

Not if *you* don't – that's for sure. I'd have no way, no way at all, of finding out. If there are resources, they'd be in your sphere, not mine. Anyway, yeah, no three pregnancies or kids are ever the same. The fact they're all from the same mother, or same family, notwithstanding.

"Notwithstanding" – what does that actually mean, anyway?

Too much to explain. Think of it as an elder cousin of "whatever."

I like the idea of everybody choosing their own name at some specified age, and having a naming ritual. I know some people do that.

Looks like that's where we are right now – and I love the idea of creating a ritual! All this time I've been thinking of you as the Strawberry, but maybe we've arrived at a "specified age." And really, if you choose a name *I* don't like, or don't immediately click with, so what? Soon that name will *be you*; it'll be your name, and that'll be that. I don't want to lean on you.

What if I were Berry, or even Straw – sounds like a clown in Shakespeare, doesn't it? One of those funny guys in *A Midsummer Night's Dream*?

Hey, either is fine, but not if you're just trying to please me. Do you *like* those names?

Oh, I'm just sort of riffing on what's already here. So: there's Berry, spelled with an *e* – that's got the nostalgia thing going, from the last thirty years, reminding us of what I looked like in the syringe.

True, but now that we're analyzing, it sounds like a boy's name – when you hear it, it's like Barry with an *a*. If you were a person, with a social security number and a photo ID, everybody would think you were a man if they heard it – it'd be gendered; it doesn't have a trans hit. Straw *is* genderless – it's got that going for it.

Yeah, but maybe it brings to mind the camel's back, and I don't want that connotation.

You think? I got chocolate malt, right away, my first word association.

(Laughing) Well, you *would*, Denah, and it *would* be – for *you*. Thing is, there aren't any rules we ought to follow – I bet even Miss Manners published no guideline for this. My situation is, as far as we know, pretty unconventional.

But she might have had something to say, something to suggest. She's flexible, smart – she keeps learning. Look, she had to come up with ideas about cell phone etiquette – if that's not an oxymoron. She might not be daunted by this.

She'd need the image – the visual. She'd need the kind of information you had. I've always thought the reason you can have this relationship with me is that you know what I actually looked like before, during and after the abortion. You knew about embryonic and fetal anatomy, *and* you had the strawberry jam image. Hey, don't you think it's cool I had a tail? Even though I couldn't do much with it – I mean, given lack of external context and such minimal physical presence. Did you think I'd be a girl back then because you *wanted* a girl?

I suppose. I thought since I already had a boy it'd be a good balance. I was so crazy about Joey, and we were so happy. Yeah, at that time, because being a conscious woman was new to me, I thought it'd be great to raise a free woman, like raising a good man. I was young and excited and ignorant – I still believed in revolution. I mean, on a national scale, like Cuba and VietNam. I know those two weren't completely successful, but still.

Cuba and VietNam! What about a country name? Russia! That's a great name, and it fits – given our ancestors and all.

What an idea! I like it. Russia! Or, given all the creepy hacking stuff, maybe we should make a list. Some for sound – you know, the beauty of it; some for family relationship; some for meaning, like symbolism – Cuba would be like that. Are there others?

India, China, Canada! Mexico, Cameroon, Persia, Egypt, Italy! This *is* a great idea! I love it! Except now it's hard to choose – there are so many.

Take your time, Honey. And think about whether the politics of the actual country will matter to you.

I don't know; I mean, governments change over time. Like, if I'm Russia, I don't have to think about Putin, I can think about Gorbachev or the early twentieth century idealists, or your grandparents – or just the land: *Mother Russia*. Or if I'm Persia, I don't need to deal with Iran's politics. I like the sound of Persia. What if we test them? Let's use one for a while and see if it works, see if I like being called that.

Fine with me; any way you want to do this is fine with me. Which one should we start with?

Knocking

... The younger generation
will come knocking on my door.
– Henrik Ibsen

Andrea's a white woman with silver-grey hair and a chronic cough. She walks a lot, mostly down the middle of Portland's small residential asphalt streets; they're easier on her joints than concrete sidewalks. She learned about that resiliency when she injured her knee in '99 and had to stop riding her bike. She became a committed walker then: no car, some buses and trains, mostly walking. That's how she gets where she's going.

She's seventy now, and it *is* terribly strange, just like Simon&Garfunkel sang it would be. She thinks of herself as an entry-level old person; she doesn't have the chops yet, not like people over eighty, but – and this is important to Andrea – she's ahead of the boomers. Born smack in the middle of that war they popped out after, them with their group identity.

Andrea got tattooed in the summer of '73, a pink ribbon with red rosebuds at both ends and the name "Jane Roe" written on it, rippling across her belly a few inches below her navel. Even later, when Weddington's plaintiff went over to the dark side, that name still meant what it was supposed to mean: Everywoman. Anywoman. Andrea.

She met the two young women in this story at the hot tubs on NE 33rd. She was lying on her back on a bench, eyes closed to the sun drying her naked skin, baking her cough, when she felt their shadows move across her face and chest. She opened her eyes and one of them said, I love your tattoo! It's so, like, vintage! The lines, you know? The style – and the meaning too, the politics. Totally.

Andrea sat up.

Yeah? She squinted. I see you don't have any yourself, though. She looked at the other young woman and said, You, however, are ahead of the game. The second one, who hadn't spoken yet, had bracelets of bright beads tattooed on both wrists, tiny golden serpents wound around both nipples, and a purple sash drawn in soft folds circling her waist.

Both of them were darker than Andrea, but she couldn't be sure, squinting in the sun, if they were women of color or simply tanned by the strong summer sun of global warming. When she'd first opened her eyes, dazzled by that light, Andrea thought – for just the tiniest second, the way you can think a whole story in what seems later like not even time – maybe these young women could be mixed-race grandmothers of the golden people she imagines will live on earth afterwards, when the horrors have subsided and remaining species are few enough to live on the little bits of air and water that're left, eating food grown in soil clean enough to be tilled in those new, post-Monsanto, years.

She squeezed her eyes shut again for a second and did a tiny head shake. Then she opened her eyes and saw them clearly: two young women, naked as she was, out there on the wooden deck of a bath house in Northeast Portland.

You're right, the first young woman said. I'm trying to decide – I'm still not sure.

Andrea swung her legs aside so they could sit down if they wanted. She said, It's a serious choice. Choosing can be hard.

The second young woman sat down close enough that her bare thigh touched Andrea's and said, No. It's only hard if you *think* it is – choosing's not a hard thing at all, by itself. I mean, the *nature* of choosing, like, making choices? People do it all the time, for different reasons, all day long, every day of our lives. *Every*thing we do makes us, like, choose one thing and not another thing. Everything's like that! Then she said, I'm Dannie, Danita. This is Andrea. She pronounced it Ahn-*dray*-uh.

Andrea! Andrea said, pronouncing it that way too. That's *my* name. Except I say *Ann*-dree-uh.

No way! Seriously? That's amazing! So, this is like Fate, right? Destiny? I was supposed to meet you today, young Andrea said, with your old tattoo and your old woman wisdom. You're going to, like, help me decide.

Andrea – our Andrea, the elder Andrea, the one this story began with – laughed. She laughed so suddenly, so loudly, she nearly barked. Oh? Is that the deal? Is that what's happening here?

Half an hour later, sitting in the tea shop on Alberta, waiting for their order to be called, the three women kept talking. Their hair was dry already.

Andrea the Younger said, Like, taking the bus or taking the train to get downtown? Getting up early to shower, or sleeping as late as possible? Those choices aren't so hard because, like, who cares? But telling the truth or a lie, telling or not telling *any*thing to your parents, your boss, your friends? That's hard! Come on – you *know* this! Some decisions are more important, *totally* more important – and *hard*. It took me like four months to decide whether to get an IUD – like, could there even *be* guys I'd want to have sex with? I spent half my senior year deciding whether to go to Colorado for college

– and I don't even know how many weeks I went back and forth about breaking up with Jess when we graduated – it's hard! And, like, what if you change your mind? What'll you do then? Because, I mean, face it, the choice you're making is just how you feel *now*, what you think *now*. How'll you feel in ten years? Or even just *one*? That's the thing, isn't it? You can't, like, know for sure.

Then Dannie said, You can't know anything for sure. I mean, are you saying we – I, you, everybody, anybody – can't make decisions at all? Because *every* decision we make, every choice we make, is what we think now, what we feel now. Because, how could it not be? These questions – what are they really about? You can't seriously be advocating paralysis, indecision, going along without making judgments – *can* you?

Andrea the Elder looked from one super-clean face to the other. She said, What matters is taking responsibility for our choices, owning them, as the shrinks say, and recognizing that everything we do, even the simplest actions, is influenced by who – and where – we are – in the world, I mean. Because we'll always have choices – all our lives! – we need our choices to grow out of consciousness. Not just whether to buy apples from New Zealand, either. I mean all the way up to the major league stuff: life and death choices.

Two months later, Andrea the Younger texts Danita: I decided! Call me!

Dannie calls her, and AtY says, I'm getting a tattoo. You have to come with me. This weekend for sure. Just one. I think. Well, two's not impossible if they're tiny. Now that I'm working out at the farm, maybe a vegetable – or some fruit? Something kind of, like, connected to growing, you know? Maybe have it coming up out of the ground, or opening on a branch? Maybe a pair of cherries? Little ripe strawberries? Two tiny oranges, like those ones we get around the winter solstice?

Knocking

Where will you go? Do you like that new place on Hawthorne? What about the one downtown, where we saw that woman playing the tambourine, the one who painted herself orange? Or the real old place on the east side – the oldest ones are totally amazing. When my roommate Marla got tattooed in Chicago, she went to the oldest place she could find – she wanted a classic mindset. I was with her. We went around Valentine's Day so she could see the most possible hearts. Their flash was, like, really old school – it was serious. This place was so old it looked like my grampa could've gone there before VietNam. Right before he shipped out he got a map of Oregon, with a little red star where Warm Springs is, on his shoulder. So, this place had valentines with Cupid-arrows stuck through – some had penises instead of arrows! Dick-hearts! Some were really frilly, and the lace looked totally real. There were shiny gold ribbons – it was cool how they could make the ink look shiny – and they had black and red that looked like they'd feel velvety. Some were torn, real jagged, and had silver tears crying out of their edges – broken hearts. It was right by the el – you know that elevated train they have there? Sorta like walking across the river on the Steel Bridge when the Max goes over? This shop was like practically underneath the tracks, and the whole place kind of rumbled – you could feel it – when a train would go over. But nobody hardly even noticed! The guy doing her valentine just lifted his needle – still buzzing! – above her skin until it faded away.

I was watching her being done and looking at all the walls. They had Mickey and Minnie Mouse dressed in black leather, and Goofy riding a Harley. They had Daffy and Donald Duck too, and they were sort of, like, having sex with a girl duck in a yellow polka-dot bikini. I remember the color of the bikini was the same color as her bill. Duckbill yellow, almost orange? They were all like cartoons from before television, cartoons from film school history class, pre-Pixar, way-early Disney cartoon shorts.

A *girl* duck? What are you saying?

Oh, Andrea! Girl, woman, whatever – it was a *duck*! Listen, they had a whole wall with pictures of women from so long ago – seriously, so old school, not the way you see women now. Hula dancers, mermaids and women wearing sailor shirts with their stomachs showing, naked witches riding on broomsticks. And all the naked women's nipples were drawn like cherries, like you see stuck on top of a banana split? It was almost a museum, that place.

Hey, let's call Andrea the Elder! It could be cool if she came with us and gave me, like, her blessing. I have her in my phone.

Wait – what? Her *blessing*? You mean, like, a fairy godmother?

Soon To Be A Major Motion Picture

Denah talks to the movie people

I remember tiny details and I remember whole scenes. Sometimes I even see them as shots, as if through a camera lens – like the scene with Sherrie, the woman I was with when we got busted: We're standing there, waiting for the elevator, and the camera is behind us – so when the doors open, the audience sees the cops in that frame. Those guys looked like they were *already* in a movie, actors playing 1972 Chicago cops: white guys, shiny black shoes, trench coats. They talked like they learned how from tv.

But here's the thing – there's a lot I don't remember. I don't remember the name of any other woman that day, just Sherrie, and I don't remember what I said on the phone when I called my husband, Eli, from the police station and got Tony, his partner. I've forgotten a lot. We'll have to invent all that – doesn't matter though, does it? There's the mystery of memory itself, for one thing. Who knows, now, what really happened that day, or might have happened? For the movie, it'll be *based on a true story*. It can't *be* a true story; that's impossible. If it's good though, I mean if we make a really good movie, it'll tell the truth.

I've got files here on my laptop – my research, a bunch of pieces I've written over the years. When we decided to meet, I put it all together, making a list of possible scenes. I've never worked on a fiction film, never wrote screenplays or treatments. I spent some time a few years ago thinking maybe I'd do it, but that did not – to put it kindly – pan out.

Now, don't be offended: I'm using this little recorder. My agent told me to do it so I'd have my own copy, audio, of what goes on here today. She said we were far enough along that I could talk freely but I should record everything. And this'll be clearly visible in your video, so we'll have a cross-referencing thing going on. After all the weeks of email and phone conversation – and seeing films you've worked on – I feel like I know you. It's probably an anachronism for me to even *care* about knowing you outside of cyberspace, but that's who I am, that's who you're working with here.

So, you don't mind if I'm sort of all over the place? After each question, I'll just talk 'til I stop? Then you'll ask more questions and I'll talk some more.

I remember two women from the holding tank, when the seven of us, the Janes, got put in with them. Even right now, while I'm telling you this, I can see both women *clearly*. It's weird, isn't it, what we remember? And what we don't? The first time I tried to write this, I didn't know who took care of the baby while I was working. Which is truly bizarre because at the time, I couldn't stop thinking about the baby. There was the breast milk situation plus fear – I was thinking: What if they take my baby away because I've been arrested? And: If I do time, he won't know me. That was in my head all day, and it was a *long* day; we started doing abortions about nine, got busted at three, got to the lockup around midnight.

Scenes and characters. It's gotta be different, thinking about scenes and characters for *film*. I mean different from writing stories and poems – what I do. Like this: the woman who fingerprinted me is the one who took me to the cell, and then, later, to see the lawyers, and down to the holding pen again, before night court – we had a miniature relationship by the end of the night, you know? Writing about her, I gave her a name, Angie, and I wrote lines for her, some from what could be memory. She was kind to me, and I made her a character. Now though, we might not have her in there at all. I need to learn from you how to think about this, how to make decisions for a movie.

For structure, form, I think of Barthelme – he has that great story where abortion docs talking about their work are mashed up with other characters at a fancy dress ball. In film, that'd maybe be Jarmusch? The messiness of it, everything happening at once – real life! It's hard enough to decide which people and scenes to use; then we have to fold 'em together to get the effect we want, the *effect* of real life. That's true in most movies, don't you think? Not just in collage forms like *Crash* or *Mind the Gap* but even the more story-telling kind. *Monsoon Wedding*!

We have to decide whether our movie is the kind where the audience knows about the bust early, or the kind where it's more like a mystery, an adventure where they don't know what'll happen. Most people *won't* know this story, coming in. It's not a piece of history people are familiar with. So do we start by giving them that knowledge? Do we use flashbacks? Maybe surround the story of the bust with other stories of the abortion service? Stories of that year and time, pre-Roe but on the way to Roe? Do we want to have a present-day moment to move back from, or is it all in the seventies? Do we want to show the time when funding got cut – the Hyde amendment, or when everybody finally recognized that Roe was now irrelevant, eviscerated? Should we show Roe going down?

Another thing, also structural, but in another way: You know how, in *American Splendor*, they did that fusion, that combination of fiction & documentary plus the combination of animation & live action? They used animation because they were dealing with a comic book person – Pekar – so it was a natural, however unusual. But other movies, that have no obvious or special reason do that too – mix methods, I mean. Like *Juno*, in the credit sequence. Oh hey, even better – better than *Juno* – is *Run Lola Run*! Structurally fascinating, structural play that never takes you away from the action, the characters. It even deepens them, really. Way tougher than *Juno*. Really, given our material, I think it's worth considering. I'm not suggesting we do anything as, like, *cubist* as Todd Haynes did in his Dylan movie. (Wasn't that brilliant?) I'm just thinking we could have some formal schtick, something structurally notable. That could be good. I don't want to make a huge case for animation – it'd just be fun. But, fact is, this is *history*, about real people, and there's documentary footage we could use. That's a good argument for fusion, don't you think? I've got that here, in case we need to refer to it.

We should probably think about doing what they did in the first *If These Walls* – when the Demi Moore character approximates the death pose from that classic photograph of a woman who had a butcher abortion. Even before they caught the Philadelphia guy in 2011, a thing like that would reverberate in the audience – that mix of fiction and reality, layering and complicating. Good movies are complicated, right? Like real life.

Some of the original characters and situations might fall away; I saw that when I was working on my own. We don't have to include everything, even in a movie about things that really happened. I am *not* suggesting we change history, though – that's outrageous. Look what they did to the history of England in the first Cate Blanchett *Elizabeth*! I am *not* in favor of that. Like, I wouldn't change the date of the bust, or the location.

Conflate characters? Maybe. Sure. When I'm doing fiction, after all, inventing characters, they're made of everything

I know – that's big conflation. Janes? You mean, would I conflate the Janes who were busted, have four or five, not seven? I don't think so. In the group, the whole Service, sure – but not the seven; there *were* seven, there have to *be* seven. That, for me, is like changing the year, the city – changing history. I once heard about a tv show using the Service. A woman I met in a bathroom line in DC at the big march in 2004 told me about it when she saw my JANE button. She said the abortions on that show were done by docs, and the docs were men – or at least one was. And the whole scene was Pittsburgh or some other place not-Chicago. Definitely out of the question.

Yeah, I *have* thought about doing those parallel tracks: Sarah Weddington and her team, working on the Roe case – not actually connected with the Service, they probably heard about the bust in spring of '72 and, like anybody who cares about this, they had to be affected by it. So they *could* be in it. I'm not saying they *should*. The Seven were definitely affected by those lawyers, their work. After all, the Janes got released on bail and their case got dropped eight months later – and why? Because of Roe moving through the system to the Court. Having our case dropped, and our records declared "expunged," that's a link between the Weddington story and ours. So it's a connection that could be used, or mentioned, in the movie. Or not.

Yeah, that's right. We always called it the Service. I know pretty much everybody who learned about us later calls the whole group JANE, or sometimes "the Jane Collective" – but *we* didn't. It was the Abortion Counseling Service of the Chicago Women's Liberation Union – which we also didn't call it. We had to shorten it – obviously – and used the one word. We did call ourselves Janes, and we played with the word, called the work "Jane-ing" and, at some point, like two years in, started calling a couple of the necessary jobs "big Jane" and "little Jane" – phone work, counseling assignments, making appointments. Lots of us did those jobs, sort of in rotation, over the years. Oh – and this: we were *not* a collective. We'll see what happens, as our work develops, whether we want to even deal with the politics of that – like how that concept got applied to the Janes by the next generations.

It's interesting how language changes. Like in the video documentary that came out in '95, one Jane (she's dead now) actually calls women who came through the Service "clients," a word un-thought of in those years, and certainly a word she, that Jane, would never have used *then*. It would have been wrong, in our thinking and practice, to separate them from us, to *professionalize* the Janes. We were too raggedy-ass for that, and committed to a way of thinking about the work that basically damns such separation. We were women who learned how to do some necessary technical work, and we understood that most women who needed that work could do it too – if they wanted to learn. Positions taken around the speculum could switch at any time. And they did. There were Janes who joined up after coming through the Service to get abortions.

Anyway. Let's set aside Women's Studies 201 and get back to the movies.

You realize I'm telling this from my own memory *and* what I've gathered from other people's memories about that time? There's no separation any more. When I decided to work on these stories again, to write more about the Service, I made a rule for myself: I wouldn't watch the video again until I was done, and I wouldn't re-read anybody's Jane writing either, until I had complete drafts of my own stories. Not necessarily polished, but complete. I wanted to draw everything up, like from a well, a pool of fluid memories. After that I could make up things – write fiction, not memoir.

When I write fiction, about anything, I'm already doing the same thing you're getting from me in this interview. I probably *couldn't* tell it all in straight chronological order anyway, so it's great you're willing to be loose. While I'm talking, things make me think of other things. I did make a list though, a rough chronology of that day – May 3, 1972. I've got it here, brought it with me. Just in case.

Thank you, yes, I'll need some water. No, no coffee. You made a good choice here. I'm so glad this big suite has that tiny kitchen. Not only do we have lots of room to spread out, we've got coffee, tea and a place to brew it.

One person who comes to mind is Francesca – I named her that, don't know if I ever knew her real name – the one who called the cops. She could be a character. I wrote a few sentences for her. She says:

> It's a sin, she can't do this. She has to have it, we all have to. Jesus doesn't want her to get rid of this baby. That's why I did it.

For the movie we could have her say those lines in court, or maybe in a scene at the police station: a Jane sees her, this woman who'd been among those waiting at the front, sees she's being talked to by the cops real intently – different from the others, you know?

We never knew if she made the call on her own or was part of a group. One way or another, most of us thought that our own cops, in the precincts where we usually worked, wouldn't have acted on her call. They never did before; this was the only bust, ever, in more than four years, and they knew all about us. They knew who we were and where we were. They knew we were good, clean, didn't hurt anybody, and weren't in it for the money. They didn't even come after us when that reporter – what was her name? I've got her in my notes – wrote an exposé for *The Reader* – you have that, right? Sometimes the cops used the Service for their own daughters, wives, girlfriends – or so I've been told.

When we were brought in, the seven of us, somebody actually said, What are we doing *here*? This isn't our neighborhood – these aren't even our cops! I was a northsider so they wouldn't have been my cops anyway, but I did a lot of time in Hyde Park for abortion work, so I knew what that meant. Those Cottage Grove guys, they were strangers.

Here's my thinking: I made up "Angie" and "Francesca" – as if I created the people, as if they weren't, hadn't ever been, real. It seemed like the natural thing to do, appropriate for fiction, melding real life (or what the writer/movie maker *thinks* is real life) with what we make up, what we invent on purpose. We're not talking James Frey here; this is not about being phony, or "lying" – in any ethical/moral sense. This is what Grace Paley meant when she said a story is a lie the writer tells in order to tell the truth.

So none of these people has a real name. I changed all the names but my own; I'm still Denah. It's simpler, easier, safer all 'round, even though I go in and out of the frame all the time in my mind. Talking about myself in the third person *can* get confusing, especially when I'm trying to be coherent for somebody else, like now.

Writing alone, before you contacted me, I decided to have the guy who sets up the bust become a character. Maybe he's got S. Epatha Merkerson's job on *Law and Order*, but in 1972 Chicago you can bet he'd be a white man. He testified that Denah lost them three times, driving from the front to the place. (I *loved* hearing him say that in court.)

If we do make him a character, I think this guy should have a conscious position on abortion. He could be something of a pragmatist, philosophically speaking. Like, he personally thinks the woman should be the decision maker, but he's an officer of the law and abortion's against the law, the Janes are breaking the law – all that.

That's different from my own cop, Denah's cop – *his* attitude about abortion I haven't decided yet, though we may not need one for him. His attitude about me, and how he decided to approach the arrest interview, is in some things I published a while back, a few years before we first talked about doing this. Have you gotten to that stuff yet? I have it here, in one of these folders.

Yeah, here's Denah-the-character and her cop: Denah's put in an office alone, still handcuffed, with the cuffs locked onto an iron ring attached to the wall. What? Yes. Really. She could sort of hear Claudia and Betsy's voices; the doors weren't closed and they were in an office next door or across the hall. She's sitting on a wooden chair near but not at a big wooden desk, and the cuffs, the metal kind, are cutting into her skin. She's at an awkward angle and her arms are raised, hanging from the ring on the wall. She'd been locked onto a similar hookup inside the police van. The office is warm, overheated in fact, but the van was cold – cold air, cold metal that made her shudder. Eight years later, when my son Joey got hit by a car and I was in the back of the ambulance holding him, I felt his body shudder that same way – police vans, ambulances, they're all cold metal, and lots of people who get put inside them are in shock. So they get that stammering kind of shiver, a hard shiver.

Anyway. So: the cuffs, the iron ring. She's sitting there thinking it's overkill, sorta medieval. But she doesn't know if it's mindlessness, meanness or strategy on their part. Her cop is sitting at the big desk, making notes, deliberately not looking at her, maybe tactically ignoring her. She's watching him, thinking about how to talk to him, what words and tone to use. And knowing definitely that soon she will have to pee.

Here's how I wrote that part:

He's wearing a yellow short sleeve dress shirt with a black knit necktie and tan pants. No visible badge. He's a white guy with bright black hair cut too short, a slightly military effect. There's a shield tattooed on his left forearm; it looks new to Denah, who got her first tattoo maybe six or eight months ago. She thinks he's a couple years under thirty, about her age. He looks up, makes eye contact. He stands, comes around the desk, takes the cuffs off the iron ring, off her.

She slumps in relief, rubs her wrists and says, I need to go to the bathroom.

He walks her to the door of a nearby women's room, waits outside. When they're back in the office, he opens a manila folder, reads silently, then looks at her across the desk – eye contact again – and says, I see you were a high school teacher. I used to be a high school teacher; I taught Biology.

She says, I taught English, Humanities and Creative Writing – but you must have all that in your folder. What made you give it up? You didn't exactly move to a higher paying job, did you? Cops and teachers, serving the public with small paychecks, right?

He laughs. He lights a cigarette and offers it to her right from his mouth. She takes it, says, Camels, my dad's brand. She puts it in her mouth, then pulls it out and says, Forgot – I'm off it.

He smiles. Then he says, Yeah, this salary isn't what they call "compelling." But you didn't move up the class ladder either, did you? We couldn't find any money at your place, and the only woman who's been willing to say *any*thing says she paid $43. I don't see you flying down to Rio on your cut. But I'll be getting a solid pension; you probably can't say the same. I guess we'll have to assume you did it for some other reason. Right?

She looks directly into his eyes. Did what?

That scene is one of the ones solidified in my mind as what happened that day. He had information about me because I was in the news in 1970 when I got fired from my teaching job.

What? Oh, the usual reasons for those years; two other teachers and I were accused, like Socrates, of corrupting the youth with our words and thoughts. Actually, the stated complaints were that we didn't follow the curriculum guide and rules about attendance and grades. It was all about politics, though; everybody knew that. Teachers were being fired all over the country, a lot of parents were freaked out – this was when the phrase "generation gap" got invented. But that's a whole 'nother movie. Anyway, our conversation was not what I'd expect to be talking about over there at the cop shop – if I'd expected to be busted for abortion, which I definitely hadn't.

Hmmm? Oh, sure, yes, the Janes talked about it, how to act, what to do; the idea was you'd never go to work without a contact number to call, but I didn't think it was inevitable, no. For sure *not*.

Sitting there, arrested on dozens of felony charges – abortion's felony homicide when it's illegal – his attention to my personal history and the revelation of his own snagged my interest. Maybe that's why he did it. Biology, I was thinking; so he must know all about this. That was silly of me, when you realize how many of them don't know a damn thing about women. But it is what I thought.

In one draft – written longhand quite a while ago – I wrote:

> The dogwood was in bloom, and the flowering plum.
> Chicago has spring for only about a week each year,
> mostly going nonstop from the darkened patches
> of snow on street corners to a sticky heat so intense
> some people sit outside on the stoop all night.

> He was wearing a necktie in the humid Chicago
> springtime, when the skin on students' arms had
> begun to stick to the pocked varnish of their wooden
> desktops at South Shore and DuSable, Roosevelt and
> VonSteuben, to the slippery formica on newer desks
> at Mather and Mother Guerin – reminding them that
> summer school was going to be hell.

> He'd been a teacher, like me, and he too had changed
> jobs. Neither of us had gone up in salary, but both of
> us were doing what we thought was *good work.*

What's interesting here is that Denah liked the guy, even
though she knew he was her adversary, dangerous to her and
the other women. She liked him as a person, *a human.*

Here's some backstory for the Denah character: She takes
time off when her baby's born, and when he's a few months
old, she goes back to work, returning to her medical training
as an abortionist and doing other Service work, sort of
part-time. She's already learned and done long-terms, she's
learning to do D&Cs. Her first full-time work day is the day
they get cracked.

Denah's the driver that day, in a borrowed Ford station
wagon, going back and forth between the front in Hyde
Park (brown brick 6-flat) and the place in South Shore (grey
highrise by the lake). She took three, four or five women
each time, using different routes, pulling over to collect the
money with each group. I have some memory fragments –

like asking them to be quiet in the hall at the place, bringing them in, and introducing them to Paula and Harriet.

Oh, here's something: There was a woman who was done, and Denah was taking her group back to the front but she said, I gotta lie down for a while longer – I don't wanna go back yet. When I get back there, to my husband, I'll have to smile and be cool, and I'm not ready to do that – you know what I mean? I don't remember her whole face, but I know she had a tiny open space between her two front teeth; I saw that when she smiled at me. She was wearing a thin grey cardigan with a rolled collar. Jeez! I haven't had that memory come up for forty years!

The thing about actually being arrested – that word is so right, if you think about how it means *stopped, held in place* – we, Sherrie and I, were certainly *arrested*.

The arrest itself, my part of it, went like this (and we should definitely use this): Denah's out in the hall with Sherrie because she asks to be taken back to the front soon as she's done. Sherrie says:

> My daughter's over in Children's Memorial today, she's only two, she's having an operation on her stomach valve. It doesn't work right, since she was born. My husband's over there, with her, for that, while I'm here, for this. Could I leave right after I'm done? Could you take me back right away? Would that be ok? Would the other women mind, do you think?

> Denah looks at her copy of the day's list and says, Sure, why not? I can do that, I'll take you back as soon as you're done.

So around three o'clock they're standing out in the hall in front of the elevator. The elevator doors open, and these men get off. Denah and Sherrie step aside to let them pass, but then – here's a place we have to make up what happened because the actual moment, the details of it, are not in my memory. Isn't that weird? You'd think that moment would be at the top of the list, but no. We don't have to worry though, because isn't that one of the most common scenes in tv and movies – that moment? You could write it with only half your IQ in gear, couldn't you? How they're arrested, stopped by these guys, these tv-type cops? And if you don't know the old procedurals, we can go back to *Dragnet* – no, no, wait, that's too early, we need whatever it was right then, 1972, to avoid anachronism. I hope you care about that. I care about that.

Were cop shows big in the late sixties, early seventies, like they are now? That was when I pretty much stopped watching tv. What *was* on then? We can find out on the Net – or in my office; I've got this great book that lists movies and tv shows and headlines and fashions and inventions and sports for almost a hundred years. The writer's friend.

What I do have in my memory (or I already made this up and now I can't tell the difference) is that soon as the initial moment of confusion passes, and realization takes hold, Sherrie starts crying. This is in the hallway, away from the elevators, where the two women are being held. Denah comforts her, puts an arm around her, tells her she doesn't have to say anything, counsels her about her rights. Hearing Denah say those things, the cops separate them, and one guy takes her downstairs because they decide Denah's a "perpetrator" and Sherrie's a "victim." Outside, Denah's cuffed and left locked in a police van. She's alone, scared and shaking inside that cold metal van the way I said before.

I have no memory of ever seeing Sherrie again – not at the station, not in court, nowhere. I sometimes wonder if they maybe let her go. She was frightened, thinking about her little girl in the hospital – and they didn't need her. Maybe they realized, with all those other people, they didn't even *need* her.

They must've had several cops and paddy wagons at the front too, for rounding up all the women who'd come for abortions, and all the mothers, sisters, children, fathers, husbands, friends and lovers who were waiting for them – my memory's got the number forty-three in it, but who knows? At the station, it seems to me, there was a fairly large open waiting area and all those people. Everybody from the front and everybody from the place was there. The children were over-tired, hungry, running around. Poor little kids.

And there was a place where we made our phone calls – maybe a bank of pay phones in a hallway? This is a period piece we're doing, might as well be *1872*, because think how different it is *now* – with abortion so recently illegal again – everybody carrying cell phones with cameras and email and text-messaging. A bust like this'll be out on the Net, YouTubed before anybody even gets booked!

So, anyway, in that open space where the phones are, the Janes all see each other for the first time since they were brought in. I don't know whether the separate interviews or the group meeting out in the open comes first – which makes sense for the movie? I do know that at first the cops weren't sure which people they'd rounded up were abortionists – "suspects" or "crooks" in their terms. In my case, since there's only one driver and they'd followed me, and then saw Sherrie and me at the elevator door, heard her cry and heard me tell her about her rights – they didn't have much to decide. But they did have to bob & weave to figure out which other women were Janes.

Some chronology: They take their wagonloads from the front and the place to the Cottage Grove station and then, after a long time there, they take us – the seven – to the women's lockup, downtown. Don't remember how we got there. Paddy wagon, wouldn't you think, another van? I have no memory of that passage. There, when we were booked, one of the guards – I think they were called matrons – was a big woman with soft skin.

She's the woman I called Angie when I wrote this part:

Angie touches Denah's elbow to steer her around. Her hair is metal-grey, blunt-cut short, and she's got a faded eagle tattoo, wings spread around her right wrist; she smells like lit cigarettes. She tells Denah how to roll her fingertips so the prints won't smudge, and hands her a coarse paper towel for the slime that gets the ink off. She hangs a numbered plate around Denah's neck when she directs her to stand still and turn sideways for the mug shots.

She guides Denah to the cells, a set-up like office cubicles at an insurance company, only this big room has a cement floor and a really high ceiling and glaring lights overhead. The cells are arranged in groups with narrow lanes between them. They have metal doors and walls, and their ceilings are like sections of chain link fence, painted black and laid down on top of metal boxes. The walls don't go all the way down; they're like the walls in a public toilet, and there's a constant draft at floor level. It's after midnight.

Angie's gruff decency is in her voice when she says, I'll put you in with your partner. She unlocks a cell and points Denah into it with her chin. Denah's puzzled until the door swings open and Linda, a new young Jane she'd met at the front that morning, jumps up to embrace her. Linda's about 18, a college student working the front her first time that day. She'd been alone in the cell before Angie brought Denah. All around them women are banging on the metal walls, wailing, screaming; their banshee voices ricochet in the big room.

Six Janes in pairs were in three cells in a row; they could talk, call out, confer and reassure each other. This is how they know one's missing. Turns out, they learn later, Harriet's parents have called the state's Republican senator, to get him to do whatever it is he does for such people in situations like this. Denah thinks Harriet must be embarrassed, and maybe frightened, to be separated from the others and alone. But she barely knows Harriet, who joined when Denah was out, having Joey.

After a while, the cell-to-cell talking over the walls stops. Linda and Denah take inventory. Their cell is maybe nine by five feet. There's a slab of wood attached to one metal wall; it's about six feet long and eighteen inches wide, for sitting – or sleeping if the luck of exhaustion shuts out noise and light. There's a filthy little sink and toilet at one end. Denah milks her breasts into the sink for relief. Their communication moves from silence to wisecracks to worries, then back to silence.

That's what I've got for that part.

Hmm? Yeah, you could say that. I *was* exhausted – and scared, angry, physically uncomfortable. I think about it this way: On that day I moved freely when I started out, traveling from north side to south side, driving back and forth between the front and the place. Then I was constrained, held – *arrested*: in the hallway of the apartment building and the police van, the office at the Cottage Grove station, the holding tank and cell at 11th and State. I was in another cell too, and in night court (a room in the building's basement, shabby but with one of those high platforms so the judge can look down on you). I got back to my own street a few hours past dawn. I think the whole experience was just about twenty-four hours – and thinking that way renders it, *that day*, almost surreal. For me.

The holding tank. Yeah, there's a story there, and I'll tell you, but wait. Here's what happened at 3am when Angie took me out of the cell. She guided me to a tiny dark room – another kind of cell. In my memory it's steel mesh, a cage. I could see guys in suits inside.

Oh, hey, listen, I have the mug shots, we can use them if we want. We got 'em when our records were supposedly expunged.

What? Well, I say it that way because I sure don't believe the Chicago Police or the federal government actually *destroy* anybody's records, especially in cases with overt political implications. I bet they had a stamp that says EXPUNGED, and a place where they stored everything stamped that way, a place for storing supposedly-destroyed files. No such worries now – data storage is forever, if you want it to be.

Those pictures – my hair was pretty long then, twisted back and clipped to keep it out of the way for work. I'm wearing levis, or maybe cords, and a dark sweatshirt, probably sneakers though I can't be sure. I know my feet were cold in that cell; a damp wind came in under the metal walls and swirled around the cement floor, moving all the time, like there was a fan somewhere, or an open window.

Thing is, my breasts had been filling since I nursed the baby that morning. I'd been assuming I'd have a chance to empty them at least once – and figured I'd be home by five or six. But I hadn't gotten to it yet when the trenchcoats got off the elevator. So when I leaned over that dirty little sink in the corner of our cell and kneaded my engorged breasts to get them soft enough to release, it'd been about sixteen hours.

Not good.

Wait a minute. Where was I going here? Ah. Right, ok, thanks – I was going to talk about what happened when Angie took me out of the cell.

She led me to a tiny dark room like a cage. It's after three in the morning and these lawyers are waiting. They stand up when Angie brings me in. One is Tony, my husband Eli's law partner, a guy I've known for years, a real sweetheart; one is Al, a nice guy who went to law school with them – very smart, well-connected; and one is Hank, who used to hit on me when Eli wasn't around. I thought, These guys must know about the baby.

I wrote this part a while ago and still have some of the draft. Denah says:

> Where's my baby? Who's with Joey?
>
> Tony immediately puts his hand on her shoulder, pulls out a chair for her and says, Eli's home. He's with Joey. She slides down into the chair, closes her eyes. Nobody says anything.
>
> Denah looks up, sits up, says, And where's Harriet? Where the hell is Harriet? Do you know she's not with the rest of us? We're all together back there except her.

They tell her Harriet's in another section of the jail and explain how Senator Percy's office has gotten a lawyer who'll work separately on her case – she will not be part of the seven for legal purposes. That's all I remember about that business and, like I said, it may not be useful in the movie anyway. Maybe it's even inaccurate. The folks who worked in the senator's office back then are unlikely to corroborate anyhow.

Al, who seems to be captain of this little team, leans forward, elbows on the table, and says, Here's the plan, Denah: We want to take you out, now, down to night court. We believe the night court judge will set low bail and let you out tonight because 1) we know the guy, 2) you're a nice white lady married to a lawyer, and 3) you're a nursing mother! Really we should need only that, but we've got all three going for us. He smiles at her.

When she doesn't smile back, he says, Point is, if we do this now, when the other Janes get to court in the morning, whoever *that* judge is will have to set low bail too – your precedent will call for it, because of our guy's decision, the night court judge.

She looks at them; they're looking at her. She can see how, even tired, they're excited. Adrenaline up, like at a demonstration. Or a football game. Hank reaches across the table to take her hand; Denah pulls back. She looks at Tony. Then she says she doesn't want to be separated from the others, says she has to think about it, says she has to ask the other Janes.

At this point, I wrote some text I almost deleted but wound up just setting aside, to use some other time – or never. It's a sub-plot thing about Denah's marriage: She and Eli had an agreement he wouldn't go out of town on days she did Service work. But he flew to NYC for the day and didn't tell her. She finds out when she calls from the Cottage Grove station and gets Tony on the phone. The marriage is rocky anyway, so there's all that. First I decided none of it was necessary for the arrest plot. Then I thought maybe I'd create a subplot for each of the seven – Harriet's got the rich parents thing going on, Paula could have a boyfriend or roommate she lied to about being in the Service – you know what I mean. Then I thought – hey, seven subplots? Totally nuts. I set it all aside, and that's where it is at the moment. But if we want any of it, I've got it.

So, ok, she won't do what they want. The men are disappointed. Denah is obdurate. Hank yells, Guard! and Angie comes to take her back.

In the hall, Angie looks at her and says, You ok?

Walking back to the cells, Denah's thinking, Claudia's a mother – she's got *two* kids. And Mandy's a mother too.

When the door clangs, Linda jumps up from the wooden bench to take Denah's hands. They stand there, holding hands, and Denah calls: Janes! Here's what's happening: the lawyers say I should come with them, now, down to night court in the basement. They think they can get me out for low bail because I'm a nursing mother.

She's embarrassed to tell them the other things Al said.

They say doing this will make low bail for all of you in the morning. I need to know what you think, what you want. Should I do it?

The four Janes in adjacent cells respond instantly, calling out: Are you crazy? Go! Go now! Of course you should go! Get out of here! Go home!

Claudia says, I'd go if I could.

Linda, who realizes she'll be alone or worse when Denah leaves, doesn't say anything. She lets go of Denah's hands.

Women in other cells shout: Who's Jane? Who's getting out? Let *me* out! Some bang on their cell walls, making sheetmetal thunder.

Angie, who's been waiting for the decision, opens the cell and takes her out again. Denah calls: I'm going! I'm going to the lawyers! If I don't come back, you'll know they were right, and the judge let me go.

Angie says, This judge has been around a long time.

And that's it, so far, for that scene. Now – here's something: the woman who was that girl, Linda, the youngest one, the new Jane Denah got put in with – if *she* were telling you this story, she'd say: Listen, Denah couldn't *wait* to get out that night, she was *eager* to leave. Linda might even think Denah suggested the idea herself. I'm not sure why I think this – some other Jane told me maybe? Maybe the Linda woman said it in an interview? I don't know, but it's what the character thinks. Even if it isn't what the real woman thinks, it works, doesn't it? So we should have that.

After all, she must've been scared, or pissed off – or both, when I left her alone in that cell. I never knew her, only in the months after the bust, when the seven had to meet to deal with the case. When I saw her, years later, she was less than interested in relating to me. Once, it was when the video first came out, she didn't even say hello when she saw me. In any case, it's good to have her perspective in contrast to mine. I was surprised by it – but there it is. Conflict! Just what all the screenwriting teachers call for. And besides, like Dylan said, To live outside the law, you must be honest.

Hey, should we use that song? Just that little piece of it? I've thought of several songs for the sound track – I've got a list. A Malvina Reynolds song, a great bit by Melissa Etheridge, something by Tupac, some ani difranco… Ok. Right. Later for that. Music later. Ok.

Anyway, here's how I ended that section:

It's so late when they finally walk out of the building that the morning papers are stacked in the lobby. The headlines on the *Daily News, Trib* and *Sun-Times* say: *Seven Women Arrested in Abortion Ring* and *Underground Abortion Linked to Women's Lib* and *Nursing Mother Arrested For Abortion*. That one has a picture of Denah from two years before, when it ran under a headline saying *Fired Teachers Called Radicals By School Board.*

I need to drink some water.

Now, here comes a part that's embarrassing, but damn, it'll be great for the movie. Instead of going right home to her baby when the judge lets her out, she has breakfast with the lawyers at a fancy restaurant by the river. I have some text for this, stuff I wrote a while back:

Leaving night court in self-congratulatory celebration mode, the guys say, Hey, let's get some breakfast! Denah, when's the last time you ate? You must be starving. Let's feed Denah!

But she's not hungry. She's exhausted. She's dulled out from stress. She doesn't answer. She stands there on the sidewalk, thick, like a bull surrounded by picadors. They urge her – they'll treat her, they'll take her someplace terrific, someplace new, great food, she'll love it.

She owes them. She knows they don't want to drive her home now; that'd shut down their triumph with anticlimax. She's in a weakened condition *and* she's flattered to be the star of their little show. The tension in her body has been ebbing, but out there on the sidewalk, she's suddenly charged with a shot of adrenaline from, from – from what? Being free in bright yellow sunlight? The exuberance of those grinning guys in their super-charged political moment? Whatever it is, she says, Yes! Let's eat! Feed me!

She may have had Eggs Benedict – or, in her case, Benedict Arnold. Oh, maybe it was thick French toast with real maple syrup – let's make it something luxurious to deepen her shame when it hits, later. I don't remember what she ate, but if we use this bit, let's go that way.

They get all the papers and read them out at the table, opening the pages over toast and bacon, butter and marmalade in little ceramic pots. She fades while they crow, quoting bits from various reporters. Her eyes are closed by the time they pay the check and she's not really awake when she crawls into Al's car, crumpling up on the back seat.

Home, she goes to the baby's room and finds him sleeping. She stands beside the crib, silent. In a few minutes, Joey wakes up, maybe from the smell of her, the smell of her milk. Nursing him, the stress drains out of her body with the milk, liquefying. It's leaving her body in palpable waves, sliding down her arms, her legs, neck and back. She feels the pulse in her fingertips, mingling with the rhythm of Joey's suckling. She hears his small breathing when his mouth falls away from her nipple.

Denah wants to be excused, wants to be *forgiven* for going to breakfast with the lawyers instead of going home. Who has the power to excuse her? Who can forgive her? Certainly not Eli, who betrayed their agreement. Not her parents. The six other Janes? She won't discuss it with them – some of them are practically strangers, after all. Maybe Joey. But he's too little, too young to exercise power that way. She'll have to do it herself – and she does, but not for a long time.

Nah. No, I don't feel ashamed of it. Now, it's so much *less*, a lesser offense, in terms of my own laws, my rules & regs for behavior. I'm *embarrassed* to tell this little story about myself (I'm happy to hand it off to a character, I will say that), but I don't feel *shame*. It was a thousand years ago and on a life scale, that breakfast doesn't weigh much; it's become a petty infraction. I've done worse, and luckily I've done better. I've done *way* better most of the time.

It could be good for the movie, though; let's see what happens as we develop the script – because, really, it's more complicated than that, the cause of Denah's shame. It's not only this thing I just told you. It's not that simple. It's connected to what happens with a woman from the holding tank scene – so let me tell that now: In my memory, when we first got to the women's lockup, we were put in a holding tank with two other women. Actually, I don't remember if they were there when we got there, or if they got put in after us. I remember noticing we were all white in there, the seven of us and the two of them, and thinking how that was against the odds in Chicago for who generally gets grabbed by the police. I have a memory of those two standing up, next to each other, then sitting down with us. I've written some pieces from that experience:

> The tank is a big cage, with benches along the sides. There's enough room for the nine of us to sit in two sets facing each other – some of us on their side, some of us across from them. The tank may have smelled like stale beer. They ask us what we're there for, and when we say abortion, they say oooh! Then we ask them. They say they were walking down a sidewalk in Uptown when the cops grabbed them and said they smashed a window and stole a tv set. They say they didn't do it. We don't say one way or the other.

Talking, we learn that one is fifteen years old and five months pregnant. She's wearing jeans and a drawstring blouse under a baseball jacket with pushed up sleeves, and we can see her recently slashed wrists. The stitches are so new the black thread's still there. She says nothing about the cuts but points to cigarette burns on her inner arms and says, I did that to show I could take it. You have to be tough and you have to prove it. She had her baby's name scratched into her arm like a jailhouse tattoo: Buddy. Even if it's a girl, I'm gonna call it Buddy, she says. That's my brother's name. He's in VietNam. She has a southern accent and skin so white her veins look bluer than her tattoo.

The other woman is tiny, much smaller than Buddy's mama, but older. And she's all dressed up, wearing heels and a long lady-style coat. She has dark red hair and dark red lipstick, and she doesn't say much. She smiles almost the whole time, and looks sleepy. Maybe she's a little drunk. Later, she's the one Denah meets in the elevator, going down to night court with Angie. She's the one who goes up in front of the judge right after Denah.

That's a big moment for Denah, what she sees and hears then. It's only a moment, but it's deep. And she's kinda stunned. See, the judge smiles at Denah, and calls her Mrs. Al does all the talking. She just stands there, in front of the high bench. Her part is to thank the judge. She thinks the judge's voice is professional-friendly, sober and kindly, like the voice of a judge is supposed to be, you know?

He says, You can go now, Mrs. Marcus. You can go home to your baby. When he says that is when he smiles.

She's dulled out from the experiences of the past 20 hours but she speaks her part.

> She says, Thank you, your honor. Then she turns away and walks toward the door with Al, who – now that Denah's free – has taken over Angie's job as elbow guide. This moment I'm talking about is maybe five seconds – not as much as ten. In that moment of seconds Denah sees with peripheral vision the small woman led to the bench, and hears the judge use a different voice. He changes his voice, like you do when you're reading out loud, like to children. He changes it to a scary voice, a bad voice.

> To the small woman, he says, You. Look at me when I talk to you.

> Denah stops walking, starts to turn. Al's touch on her elbow turns to a grasp, pinching her skin through her sweatshirt. He pulls her forward and she moves with him; she walks out the door with him.

See – she left the Janes up in the cells and the small woman down in the basement. The breakfast is almost superfluous. It's symbolic – no, wait, what am I saying? No symbolism needed. We'll do it so the audience sees her *get* it, sees her understand what just happened. We need a *really* good actor for this – among the younger ones, who could do it? Jennifer Lawrence?

Right. Yes. Yes yes yes – I'll keep my cast notes with my music notes. It *is* like the music for me, because my mind just goes there, and I start making a list. For the actors it's who've I seen recently, who's the right age and type – and who's got the chops.

Let's have a tea break – I'll put up the kettle on that stove-top; is there any ginger tea in that basket of herbals?

While the water boils, let's think some more about the underneath stuff, the not-plot stuff. I've been thinking about some questions we need to answer: Should we have post-bust action in the movie? Do we want anything about what went on in the Service after May 3, 1972? How the other Janes dealt with it? What happened when the Roe decision came down? How much – if anything – do we want to do with the larger context, the whole scene around abortion in the USA at that time?

We seven, called "The Abortion Seven" in the newspapers, spent the next few months going through interviews with lawyers, and then working with the lawyer we chose. I have some of those scenes written, but they're scanty. In those months we learned about law, not medicine. Meantime, the Service kept working.

What do you think? Do we want to have those interviews, the little batch of political lawyers the seven women go to see? Each was a story all by itself – we're talking Boccaccio here, *Dubliners*. Flannery O'Conner. Alice Munro! All stories, all the time.

And do we want the one they chose, the Janes' lawyer, to be in the movie? *She* was cinematic. Picture this: She comes to court in canary yellow pants & a canary yellow sleeveless sweater, carrying a canary yellow patent leather briefcase. This is a white woman with a deep tan on her bare arms, and the arms are ringed with silver bangle bracelets; she's wearing matching bangle earrings. I wish I could remember the shoes. Anyway, she was the proverbial sight to behold and, except for us – a pack of smart girls – she was probably smarter than everybody else in the courtroom. Also tougher. So if we need a character, she definitely *was* one. Also, choosing her was not unanimous, though a grudging consensus was reached – some Jane-on-Jane tension, with Betsy against, Denah for, and a certain amount of negativity in the negotiations.

Another possibility: The Janes took a weekend retreat about a month after the bust – the seven were invited to use a farm up in Wisconsin to decompress and hang out for a few days. Now, in the world of subplots, this is probably too far out, but the fact is – I mean, the *truth* is – in real life the farm was owned by a married couple, and the man had been Denah's lover.

Yeah. Well, you know – *real life*. I'm sure it seems bizarre, or at least unreal, as reality so often does when you tell it as a story, after it's all done happening. You can imagine people in the theater saying, Sure. Right. *Please.* But the farm as a scene, a set – that could be useful, no? I mean *if* we decide to go past the bust itself in the chronology of the film, *if* we tell more about the seven in those subsequent weeks? That's why I say we have to answer these questions in front.

Thanks! This tea is lovely, so fragrant.

Here's what else I've got, in notes or full story drafts (I've got characters, plot and dialogue for some of these): some Janes who weren't working that day hit the ground running when they heard, raising money for bail, organizing, figuring out where the women could go who weren't done yet (that day and the rest of the week and the next; we had a couple hundred women waiting) – they did all get done, you know. Every single woman got her abortion.

Plus, I wrote a little about the home front – like, what's going on in the lives of the seven while the bust/jail/lockup stuff is happening. And I made up stories for several people waiting at the front, thinking about the three I already mentioned (Francesca and Sherrie and the woman who needed to rest a little before she went back to her husband) plus a typical mix of folks who'd be there – you could probably guess.

And I've got a little bit about the people who'd given their apartment to use that day – every day we worked, people had done that, you know, gone away for the day so we could use their homes – and I made up a story about *those* people, what happens when they find out the Service was busted at their apartment. Which definitely broadens the focus, maybe even diffuses the impact. I just want you to know I've got it – I want you to know everything I've got here, so we can use it if we want to. It's all potential material – stuff that could go under the credits, could be flashback, split-screen, outtakes for a DVD, whatever. Maybe we'll do a mini-series!

Oh hey, there was this guy, a *Daily News* reporter, a totally decent guy, who spotted Denah's name in the police report on the abortion bust and remembered her from the teacher firing. He'd done a long feature then, interviewed her and the other teachers – and wrote a good article with several follow-ups, a *newspaper* mini-series. So he called her.

He'd been in the courtroom that morning when the other six appeared before a different judge and things went pretty much as Al said they would. He asked me if I'd talk with him or if I'd rather talk to a woman this time. Honest to god, that's what he said! Kinda mournfully but sweetly: I suppose you want to talk to a woman reporter for this?

Yes! There was that time, that tiny time in history, my young friends, when such a thing could and did happen. I said yes, he said ok, and a few minutes later a woman called me, saying, Charlie Atwood just gave me your number; will you talk to me about the Abortion Seven?

More tea, yes; thanks.

Years ago I wrote a pair of scenes, one at a front and one at a place, running parallel in time, but I may have junked it – I can check. In any case, we could certainly put in a little of that for, let's say, a couple minutes max, before the cops show up. Then we could go right into the bust action. That's one option – it'd be easy to recreate, or we could write some new people. No matter what, we should decide how much clinical action to use and how to show it. *If* we show it. Do we show a gamut? Or just some samples? Or what? And when? Like, maybe Denah goes in to see if Sherrie's done, so there's a naturally revealed room where an abortion's in progress. We don't want to pander or sensationalize – and we sure don't want to make the mistake that Romanian director made with the fake-looking fetus, the one bad shot in a good movie. I'm assuming you've seen all the relevant films, *Vera Drake, Cider House* and the more recent ones? There's only a handful – so few you could watch them all in one day. Now, why do you suppose *that* is?

Here's a bit I wrote and never could decide where to put it – I think we should use it; it could work for us because it's dialogue. See if you like it, in the police van or at the station, Betsy says:

> 'Member that meeting when everybody was all up in arms about South Side Sam, the guy with the speculum collection? Was that when Lucy said "life is a movie"? I know, if *my* life is a movie, I'm not the director. I must be the screenwriter, because my ideas, and my lines, always get changed and cut. I definitely did not write *this* into it. These hours with the Chicago police would not have been on my list of things to include in the script of my life.

Betsy has always had some excellent attitude.

Let's talk – at some point – about how much we might need of that kind of thing, dialogue among the seven, emotional interaction among the Janes, stuff that shows how Betsy doesn't much like Denah but understands that her dear friend Claudia does – and her good pal Lucy does too. We might use the rough deal Mandy has going on, where one of the heavies doesn't like her – no, wait, that actually doesn't matter here! I'll save that for other stories; Mandy's situation as a Jane doesn't play in the plot of the bust, not really. In fact, I bet being one of the seven upped her status in the Service. And besides, I'm going too far into reality – we don't need exclusively real stuff in the movie, so we can make up the relationship parts. Harriet, and her separation from the others, for instance, whatever they think of her and she of them, can just grow out of the plot – we don't need my memories or anybody else's for that stuff.

What if we take a break? Not just a few minutes like these water and tea breaks – I think we should go for a walk, eat food. Are you up for that, or is it just because I'm talking so much I need to change gears? I know you two must be really tired, coming right from the airport, setting up, and then being on the receiving end of all this talk. You should rest too. Let's turn everything off and get out of here for a while. Let's walk over to the lake.

Nice work on your forearms – I especially like the moon and stars, the way the color was done. Where'd you get it?

Mine was all done here in Chicago except one; this one I got in San Francisco from Lyle Tuttle. All of it long before you were old enough to get tattooed, maybe even before you were born. *I love saying that!* I don't just mean the deliberate use of cliché (enjoyable as that is). I once met a woman on the bus, about as much older than me as I am older than you. She sat down next to me. After she got settled in, she leaned over and looked me over. All over. Then she grasped my thigh, and squeezed. Then she twisted sideways to look right into my face, and said: I was getting tattooed before you were born. When the great ones – the inventors of tattoo art in the United States of America – were still working. You know what I mean, girlie?

That really happened.

Keesha and Joanie and JANE

Characters, Dialogue and Conflict Including
Opinions, Memories and Strategic Planning Filled
With Hope, Disappointment and Inspiration

Why should we wait? We know what we need to do.

Ah, you say that like it's easy, Keesh, like it's simple.

No. I say that like it's *true*, like it's obvious. Like it's what we already know. It's not gonna be easy, but we know we have to do it – we knew it the minute the Court's decision was announced. We're post-Roverturn now. We knew it was coming, and here it is. We can do it like homework, Jo: We look at the video again, read the book again, get all that other stuff we keep saying we'll read – the sociologist interviews, the senior thesis from Bard. It's a bibliography! And movies – yeah, it's Abortion Film School: *Cider House Rules* and *Citizen Ruth* and the first *If These Walls Could Talk. Vera Drake* and that heavy Romanian one - *Obvious Child* and *Grandma. Dangerous Remedy*! Hey, it's more than a bibliography; it's a syllabus. And we can read the Barnett bio for inspiration – like people read their Bibles, you know? That woman never came off it.

Should we start with just the two of us? What about some other women from the Coalition? … Do you want tea? I'm going to have some ginger root.

Yeah, sure, thanks… That's how *they* started, isn't it? Wait – no. When they started there was really just one – and she did it from her dorm room, too. Shit, she was way younger than us.

Yes, but, two things: one, we don't have to do it the same as they did, and two, even if we wanted to, we couldn't because it's all different now – the Net, cell phones, everything – there's all this ease of contact. Ease of being spied on for sure. Besides, you *know* there are other women thinking about doing this, maybe right here in Portland. We don't have to be alone. For all we know, some other women are already *doing* it. That's something to think about – like, what if somebody's already doing it?

You think we're late to the party? No – we'd have heard about it, for sure.

I know we don't have to do it alone, but how do we know who to trust? We can trust each other, but other folks could punk out, or even turn us in.

Turn us in! Whoa! That's a heavy judgment, Keesha. I mean, like, who're we talking about? We're not even sure who the others *are* yet – so let's not assume we won't be able to trust them, whoever they are. Anybody we'd ask to a meeting would be somebody one of us knows well enough to risk, right?

Hey, all's I'm saying here is we don't have to start with a full team. I'm thinking we create the set-up, and then we talk about it with other women we already trust – one by one, women we think might want to do it and might be good at it – some of it, anyway. Everybody doesn't have to want to do all of it, or be good at all of it – *they* weren't… Is there honey? Did you finish the lemon?

They're both here… What about the idea that people need to be in from the jump in order to feel ownership?

I can't get into that word, Joanie. My dad went crazy when he heard George Bush say that – I was still young enough that I lived with my folks, and I remember. Bush said the whole country should be an "ownership society," talking about owning houses, buying stocks and what-not. My dad jumped up and screamed at the tv.

Oh, but Keesha, you know what I mean – call it whatever you want. Isn't that important, even crucial? People need to be part of the plan, part of *making the plan*. It's a power thing, too; I don't want my friends thinking I need to be top girl.

Look how it happened with them: once they got going, they took in little bunches of new women a couple times a year – and those women joined up with whatever it was then; they didn't need to be in from the start, they accepted how the group was then – whenever – or they didn't join.

Yeah! And didn't the first Jane start – that one who took the calls in her dorm room – didn't she start a group when she realized she couldn't handle the work all by herself? Didn't she start by asking for volunteers at a meeting? We could do that. We could do that at the meeting of the Coalition in June, when the med students and nursing students come; I think some midwives are coming this time too.

Oh, I wish we knew *them*, even just one of them! One tough Jane's all we need. I wish we knew where they are. Where *are* they – I'm gonna say it – when we need them?!

I bet there's women all over this country thinking the same thing right now – I bet, like, those women are surrounded! There's a line of women outside every Jane's house!

Nah. I bet hardly anybody even knows who they are. Not everybody's into this like we are. There *isn't* a line. I mean, what if, even where the Janes are known, people are too scared? Or seriously traumatized by anti-abortion violence? What if we really are a tiny minority?

No way! Think about it! You were at that march in 2004! It was huge – biggest ever, bigger even than the one for Dr. King's dream speech, more people than Vietnam. And now, all the marches against Trump! That old guy, the ranger in uniform we talked to, 'member, at the Lincoln Memorial? He saw all of 'em – and he said ours was totally the biggest. And it was still legal then.

But how many of those people'd be willing to break the law? Marching is one thing; but committing a crime, systematically and repeatedly – that's something else.

Women did it before – they'll do it again.

What if the Janes are done with it, Joanie? Like that blonde in the video: "It was over for me" – she made me mad!

Wait, no – she said "once it was legal" she "passed the torch." She didn't know when they made the movie that torch'd be coming around again, real fast, real soon.

So: The Janes. They're middle-aged, or even old, but they're not dead – oh, maybe some *are* dead, but not all of 'em – there must be some we could find.

Yeah, why don't you search for them online, see what you get?

You think that's a joke, but I'm going to do it – here goes. Wait. Wait wait wait – yes! Hey! Look at all this! I'm scrolling past what we already know – ok, it's not exactly an address book – but it's a list of leads.

We can start with some of the women in the video who used their own names – and this time we take notes. And the woman who wrote the book, Laura something – and the Chicago Women's Union website probably has names – do you see any there? And one of the Janes in the old video is a writer – I bet we can find her. Somebody at the January meeting said she lives out here now, like, somewhere in Washington, or Oregon?

How about we find the women who made that video? *They* found a bunch of Janes. That was, like, twenty-five years ago? The videomakers found them – twenty years after Roe!

Uh-oh. I bet some of them really *are* dead. Almost all of them have to be pretty old. Even the youngest ones, like, let's say somebody was eighteen in 1972, now she's way over sixty – and the older ones – oh, jeez. And how can we be sure these women even think about this stuff anymore?

Girl, *every*body thinks about this stuff – that's why even if you're running for the library board in East Nowhere Nebraska, you have to tell the voters what your position is on abortion. D'you think these women, who fucking *did* it, underground, have never given it a thought since then, especially now – when it's illegal again? You think they aren't wondering about doing something? You bet they're thinking about it – they've *been* thinking about it, and now it's time, for them just like for us. Some of them, anyway.

Ok ok ok. Right. Yes, you're right. I like lost my mind for a second, that's all. If this whole thing wasn't so horrible – and if the setup work didn't need to be done like yesterday, I'd say we need to have some kind of written introduction, something to hand them with our contact information on it, something that gives them an outline of our ideas? But we don't want any of that floating around the country on paper, or buzzing around in cyberspace. We're not doing this thing on Facebook.

These are women who understand the need for secrecy. They'll be cool. But in other ways, there could be issues. Word is they were basically all white, middle class, straight – married even – and not especially political outside of the abortion underground. How will that play? Our crowd is way mixed, in all of that. And hey – I wonder if any of them turned – you know, went over to the other side, like the *Roe* woman did?

I've thought about that – not the turning, the other stuff. But, you know, maybe they weren't. We can't be sure. How 'bout that dykey one in the movie? The one in the flannel shirt who talks about how it was cool to do illegal work? She *couldn't* be straight and married. But, ok. What if we just do it without them? Let's think for a minute here. After we do the homework, just knowing what they did could be enough, like knowing the history of the Underground Railroad and what Harriet Tubman did, or the partisans in WWII, or the Warsaw Ghetto uprising. So – alone – I mean without them – how would we start? Call up doctors and say, Hey, now that abortion is illegal again in this country, will you break some laws to do it anyway?

I don't know any doctors well enough to say *that* to them; but what about med students, nurses, doulas and midwives – all those "pro-choice" people we already know? There's a woman who lives near my cousin Rhonda – oh, but she's a dermatologist. Hey, my aunt Lallie is a nurse!

How about we each make an appointment with a doctor or a nurse or a midwife, and when we get in to see them, we sort of, like, interview them? We might have more luck with the alternative types – naturopaths, chiropractors, acupuncturists – they're probably more open-minded to begin with; I heard acupuncturists can do it with a special needle pattern. Should we use fake names? Do you think we'd have to pay much for a visit just to talk? Oh, in this fucked-up medical system, probably.

What about supplies? How would we get all that? Remember what we learned from that Massachusetts woman two years ago? And Dr. Gomperts, online! About misoprostol already being used in other countries – India, someplace in Africa – alone, without mifepristone. And herbalists! We have to find the most recent info about how much to use, what's safe. Like with pennyroyal – really effective but seriously dangerous, even lethal. Maybe we can have herbalist backups like the Janes had doctor backups. And remember the woman who talked about Filipino abortion massage? Let's find *that*.

Yeah. But in the meantime, we keep looking for the Janes and – how about this? When we find them, we apply for that grant, the one for women's history month, and we use the money to bring them here, to meet women here, and the women they meet here will be, like, the ones we'll already be talking to about doing it – starting with women we know from the Coalition.

A *grant*? You think we can get a *grant* for this? Tell me what drug you are on.

I am totally, totally, totally serious. These women are historical figures. They are discussed in textbooks. They are in college research papers and high school term papers. We can hook up with some women's studies people at Lewis and Clark, at PSU, maybe PCC, Reed. So we write a grant to bring Janes here as, like, "living history" or some shit like that. We don't *say* we want them to teach a new generation of underground abortion workers. I wouldn't put that in the "describe your project" section, no.

That could work! I mean, hey, it's absolutely worth trying.

Months later, in March of 2021, drinking ginger root tea at Keesha and Joanie's house, Annie says, Technically, the grant funds a series of multi-generational meetings about women's health. These three Janes are sixty-something and over seventy – and they're speaking at local campuses. They've also been scheduled to meet with representatives of community groups. That's us.

The women Annie's talking to are members of the Portland Reproductive Justice Coalition. They're waiting for Keesha and Joanie to get back from the airport, where they've gone to pick up three Janes.

Annie's come right from her job at Trader Joe's, and she's still wearing her tropical flower shirt. Gloria asks, Do they give you those shirts for free, or do you have to pay for them? Only time I ever got handed a job uniform without it being docked from my pay was when I was a chambermaid.

I guess Trader Joe has a lot in common with the motel industry; they give you as many as you need! You just go in back and take 'em. This one cashier I met is selling them on eBay for ten bucks a pop; *he*'ll be gone soon. Anyway – they have a bunch of styles, shirts and sweatshirts. It's a great place to work, I think because they're trying to make up for having been bad about GMOs – and they don't want us to actually think about the fact that their whole deal is to source everything from so far away – and they wrap almost everything they call "fresh" in plastic. For a giant international corporation, TJ is amazing – so smart and funny and charming that even here in The City of Buying Local, people don't seem to notice what that store is actually *doing*.

Hey! Our new abortion service should have shirts that say JANE! Wouldn't that be cool?

Yeah, Letta, that'd be cool, sure – why not just call the cops and tell them what we're doing? Better yet, call the antis – they can have shirts too; theirs can say anti-Jane, you know, like anti-Christ? They'd be into that.

Oh, please, Bernie – I'm not stupid. But I do want the shirt. I won't wear it outside. We'd just wear our shirts while we're working – you know, like hospital scrubs. Over the pocket, they'd *all* say JANE.

Everybody laughs.

Jill says, *I* think we should have tattoos – maybe the name JANE in a heart, like a valentine? Or a speculum with JANE in teeny letters on the handle? They don't have to be all the same; like the Trader Joe shirts, there could be a series, different styles with one theme. This is why we need meetings – I never would've thought of that without the shirt conversation.

Hey, I promise you all, my mother's the only person I'll show my shirt – or tattoo. She's the first person who ever talked seriously about abortion with me.

Your *mother*?! That's beyond lucky – how'd that happen? Is she a feminist? An activist?

Actually, she's not, but it's a great story – and it's got a happy ending; I could tell it while we wait.

Yes! Tell! Tell! Tell us a story, Letta.

Ok, here we go: When I was in high school and ignorant as shit but starting to think – just starting – something really bad happened; I can't remember now which awful thing it was, maybe a clinic bombing? And I asked her if she'd ever had an abortion (this was when it was technically legal but really tough to get).

No way! You asked your mother *that*? Yow! Not much like the conversations in *my* family!

So she goes, Well, as a matter of fact, yes. I did have an abortion, when I was fifteen. Fifteen! I almost lost it when she said that! And I never did tell your grandma and grandpa. Then she asks me, Do you want to know about it, Letta? Maybe if I tell *you*, that'll make up for my not telling *them* – do you think that could work? My mother is a little bit into magical thinking.

So I say yes and she opens with: I was scared. And my boyfriend – he was sixteen – was scared too. I couldn't believe my mother was saying this. They used rubbers from the gas station men's room – they didn't call them condoms then. They thought they were being careful, so they couldn't believe it, waited more than three months to be sure. Over three months, then four, still no blood.

Bernie says, Whoa! Sixteen weeks! People always carry on about how young girls "wait so long" – your mother's a great example: classic teenager.

You know, my grandparents didn't speak English very well – they came here not long before my ma was born. But here's the thing: Her cousin went to college in Chicago, where they lived then, and she – Ellie Lee – was a big hero to my ma. One day she came over, looked at my mother, and knew. She just knew.

They went, my mother and her cousin, for a walk. In the park, she put her hand on my mother's little pregnant belly, looked in her face and said, What about this, Cora? My ma says she burst into tears. So Ellie Lee makes a phone call – we're talking public phones here, phone booths – and they tell my grandparents they want to take a ride in my grandpa's car. They go to a bank in the suburbs and then to a big pink motel by the highway to the airport – it's still there; I've seen it when I visit. It's really funky. In a room there was a man wearing a white coat – like a doctor's coat, my ma says – over his sweater. She says he had an accent, maybe Indian or Pakistani. He told her to lie down on the bed, and he put in a speculum.

She said the man's hands were warm and smooth; he smiled at her and said, There now. There now. When she got to this part, I was afraid she was going to tell me something awful – you know, like in that Romanian movie? – but no. He was totally excellent.

Ellie Lee held my ma's hand when he squeezed a tube, like toothpaste, up inside of her. She didn't understand the paste went into her cervix, so she thought: What'll happen when I stand up? Will this stuff run down my legs? Will everything slide out now?

• *Jeez, that's just what I would've thought when I was fifteen.*
• *Is there any fifteen year old who'd know what the hell was going on with that?*
• *You think they teach anatomy in those abstinence programs?*
• *Come on – even a kid who knows what's down there would be freaked out. Go on, Letta!*

But nothing happened when she stood up; she just stood there – and the man said to her: Drink orange juice. He and Ellie Lee talked for a few minutes, and she must have given him the money; then he went away.

When they took the car back, Ellie Lee told my grandma she wanted to take her cousin to visit her dorm for a day or two – So Cora can see what college is like, she said. Her roommate was gone, must've been spring break. Lucky! My grandma said yes because she wanted my ma to grow up to be like

Ellie Lee, go to college and be a real American. They packed up a few clothes; when she kissed her parents goodbye, they were laughing. They said, Go! Be a college girl!

They took the el across town. They bought oranges. They went to a dime store and bought what Ellie Lee called supplies, and she told my mother what was going to happen. Ma said she wasn't scared, and thinks – now – she maybe just didn't get it, you know, couldn't let herself understand? *I think she just trusted her cousin.*

They walked up the stairs to Ellie Lee's room; it was on the eighth floor – she says she actually remembers the number, 803. Then they walked down again, and Ellie Lee took the elevator back up but told my ma to walk up and down a few times, and she did, but nothing happened.

They both woke up early the next day, and ma was going to do the stair thing again, up & down, up & down, but then it started. She said it felt like her period, cramping. So Ellie Lee right away opened the supplies – newspapers, plastic wrap and dish towels, and told my mother to run in place and hop, one foot to another, back and forth. When the contractions got stronger, she had her get down on the floor. She braced her back and told her when to push. Basically, Ellie Lee was my mother's midwife for that induced miscarriage. Can you believe they did this?

• *Pretty amazing. I have some cool cousins, yeah, but would they come through for me like that? Not so much. Well, to be fair, even if they wanted to, would they have the resources?*

• *Or the connections! How did she even* know *that guy?*

• *You don't know what people will do – or who they know – until it happens.*

• *Do you know her well, Letta? This cousin? What's she like now?*

She's dead. I never got to meet her. Leukemia – there were a few remissions but she died pretty fast. When I was a kid I couldn't understand what it meant when my mother talked about her – you know what it means when people say they "long for" something? "Long" to be with someone? That's how it was with my ma when she talked about Ellie Lee. When I was a kid, I was jealous. When I was twelve, maybe thirteen, I said, you love Ellie Lee more than you love me, and she's even dead!

- *NO!*
- *Get out!*
- *You didn't!*
- *Jee*-zuss!

Yeah – I did. Please, don't *even* say it. I know. I think of what I did every time my own kid talks mean to me – which he hardly ever does, but still –

Hey! Finish the story! Come on!

Ok. Ok. So there they are: Ellie Lee who's just turned twenty and my ma who's about fifteen and a half with a four-month fetus and a dozen oranges in a college dorm room with the door locked – and it's spring break.

Think about how many girls and women have done stuff like this – thousands, right?

Bernie, I bet it's thousands of thousands – and lots of their stories don't have sweet endings like this one. You know it's happening right now, while we're talking.

Go *on*!

She says when it came out Ellie Lee spread a dishtowel over it, and then they had to deal with the placenta. It didn't come out with the fetus, so here's where they could have gotten fucked up – but they didn't! Together, they massaged my mother's belly 'til pretty soon Ma felt a big contraction and pushed her fists down hard. The placenta slid out onto Ellie Lee's newspapers and plastic wrap, and they stared at it. They just stared at it, she said.

Then they laughed. They actually laughed, both of them. Thing was, it looked like liver, like the meat their grandma used to rub with salt, and fry in chicken fat. They, both of them, never ate it. My mother was proud when the relatives all said, Cora's just like Ellie Lee, she won't eat liver. So there they are, shrieking and giggling and gasping, pointing at it, saying, It's liver! Oh my god, it's *liver*, like grandma makes! They couldn't stop laughing, she said. They laughed the whole time they cleaned up, and all the way back home, on the platform and on the train.

Then they cried. Get this: they sat down on the curb at the corner of my grandparents' street – there's a Vietnamese restaurant there now – crying, sobbing, until it was all out, all over. They were hysterical, she said, and I believe it. Clinically hysterical, I'd say. They laughed and they cried until everything was all out of *both* of them.

- *Wow – what a story! What a conversation to have with your mother!*
- *I'd love to talk to women older than me about how it was, long ago.*
- *Well, you're gonna get a chance in about five minutes.*
- *What'd you say when she told you this story, Letta?*

I asked her if she was sorry she did that – growing up as I was, surrounded by anti-abortion thinking, where the default "choice" when you're pregnant is childbirth. She said No. She said, I've never regretted it, never. Sometimes I wonder what my life'd be like, if I'd had that baby when I was fifteen – but I'm never sorry. I'm glad.

Then my not-political mother says to me, But there is one thing. I got *angry* when I got old enough to realize what the hell that was all about – and I'm *still* angry. The danger! The risk! And now, with all this terrible business with the clinics (it was the nineties when we had this conversation) and the few brave doctors, and how it's being restricted – especially for girls, girls like I was. The two of us had to do that hard, hard thing in secret! That makes me *angry*.

The door opens; Keesha and Joanie walk in with three women, all of them decades older than the women talking about Letta's mother.

Joanie says, Here are our guests.

Keesha says, pointing to each one, This is Betsy Sutton, Claudia Nowicki and Lucy Fish. The Janes smile and nod when she says their names.

The younger women stand and introduce themselves: Annie Jefferson, Gloria Gutierrez, Letta Rosenfield, Jill Owens, and Bernice Lim, who says, Call me Bernie.

Keesha and Joanie wave their hands like third graders – Keesha Wells and Joanie Karlin.

Gloria says, Welcome! Thank you so much for coming! We really appreciate it. Let's go right to the table – we can start the conversation while we eat supper; you must be pretty hungry.

The Janes push their wheeled suitcases into a corner, drop their coats on top and come to the table, where the young women have arranged plates, glasses and potluck offerings: meat, vegan and veg dishes, dark bread covered with seeds, blue and yellow corn chips and brown rice crackers, sajiki and guacamole, bottles of beer, wine and fizzy water. The Janes smile. Everybody sits down to eat.

Passing the food around, tasting and chewing and telling each other how good everything is, the older women ask questions and the young ones describe the Coalition – a group working on responsible pregnancy decisions across a wide range of medical and political skills and interests. The young ones, Keesha and Joanie and their friends around the table, have been especially interested in abortion access for a long time, since the years when *Roe* was eviscerated, even before abortion was made illegal again.

The Janes say how much they've been traveling since the overturn, and how much work is being done, including some that's underground – all over the USA. This is the first Women's History Month since the Court decision, so they're wildly busy. Annie asks, Where's Denah Marcus? The writer? We thought she'd come to this meeting; we heard she lives somewhere near here.

Yes, Lucy says, she does – not far from here, if I've got Portland's neighborhoods right; she's in Chicago this week! Funny but true. She's working on a movie about the Service, and it turns out she has to be in Chicago right now. You can talk to her anytime, though, now that you know she's out here. She's really sorry to miss this chance to meet you.

Will you give us her number? It'd be great to be able to hook up with her.

She's in the phone book, honey, Claudia says.

The phone book! Jill laughs. I don't even know where mine is. She's instantly abashed, embarrassed at having called attention to one of the obvious differences between the two groups of women. Next up, Joanie's thinking, after age will be race. And who, she wonders, looking around the room at her friends – in their textbook diversity like a WWII movie cast – who will ask about sexual identity?

But the older women smile, and Betsy says, The older you get, the longer your list of potential methods. Discard nothing, keep collecting.

When everybody's half-way done with dessert (banana cake, banana gelato, and a sticky batch of fried bananas with shredded coconut – a luxury in honor of the imminent end of banana farming), Joanie and Keesha exchange a melodramatically meaningful look across the table, and start talking like a tag team.

They tell the Janes, at much greater length than this paragraph, that they want to start a new abortion service, based on the long-ago work done underground in Chicago and modified for the 21st century. All the young women talk – their excitement rising as they offer ideas, ask and answer questions.

Then, in a sudden moment of quiet, they ask the Janes to work with them – and each Jane says, No. Each says it distinctly; all three say it definitively. They look at each other with interest, hearing these demurs spoken out loud for the first time. At none of their other jane gigs (all arranged and attended by young women like these, smart and avid, tough and bold) has anyone asked them all, straight-up, to do it. So they've not, until now, had to answer, had to decide. They all say, in one way or another but in brief: No. I'm not going to do this. I can't do this.

Come *on*! Don't tell us you can't do this! You did it before, do it again – join up; we need you, says Jill.

Claudia holds up her hand. That was long ago and far away, babycakes – and besides, why us? There's hundreds of docs, nurses, midwives who could do it, and some of 'em have done it more recently, way more recently, than we have – less than a year ago, *legally*. You think I remember everything? Decades later? You think I've done so little since then my mind isn't stuffed with other action, other information? You think my knees, these pudgy creaky cranky knees, are gonna bend down like they used to, so I can look into a few dozen vaginas every day – and then help me run away when the cops show up? You need somebody young! Somebody elastic! You can do it. You're all younger than my *kids*.

She raises her voice, a little, to say, And really, it was different then. The anti-abortion movement didn't exist, hadn't yet done its job of changing language and minds in this country, hustling up and maintaining the post-*Roe* backlash that's now our national anthem. People thought, and talked, differently then. Even us. Really! You grew up through this; you're the ones to take it on, make it happen. We'll tell you everything you want to know, though – we are not without opinions.

Everybody laughs.

Betsy says, But, like the phone book, what *we* say won't necessarily be what *you* use to get what you need – to get what you want. Miserable as they are about women, the Rolling Stones were on to something.

Everybody laughs.

Actually, Bernie says, we know that? And I bet we can even name times and places, in *our* own lives and work, when it was "different." Like, in some towns, clinic defense is – or used to be – almost simple: We signed on to be escorts and some of us didn't even need to wear bulletproof vests. It *was* different then!

Everybody laughs again.

Lucy says, I learned in the late seventies – maybe '79? – learned suddenly, in one night, how different it was, how it had already begun to change. Different from Jane-time, before and when *Roe* was decided, and different from that tiny time – only a few years! – when abortion was available to everyone who chose it, legal and safe in the US of A. In those few years before the Hyde amendment, Janes were invited to talk all over the place, mostly colleges and community groups, but high schools, too. I once talked at Mother Guerin, a Catholic high school for girls, about women's health and sexuality. The teacher, a nun, was right there with me. Then, this night I'm talking about in the years when the antis were bulking up their street power after Hyde, students invited me up to Madison to talk about the history of contraception and abortion access – sorta like some parts of this Portland trip actually, and some other gigs this year too.

What happened? Bernie asks.

This was when I – not just me, lots of us – still didn't realize the antis were going to get such an insane amount of media coverage for every move they made and every word they said. And we sure never guessed the coming rise of right-wing radio! So I was really surprised when I got off the bus at the student union building and the first thing I saw was a line of people waving signs, protesting me being invited to talk. Some of them had babies and little kids with them. I remember the babies and little kids because you could tell they were upset – by the vibe, you know? Some were even crying. Anger and menace don't play well with the tiny people, and they definitely get anxious when the angry menacing people are their own parents. The protestors didn't know who I was when I got off the bus and went through their line to go inside, so I could walk slowly, read their signs and listen to what they were saying. I even took one of their leaflets. When I read it, I was shocked at the ignorance, or maybe it was deliberate lies – and I was blown away by the rhetoric. They were scary, and I was scared.

Later, when it was over, they did know who I was, since some of them came in to listen and yell at me. So the students who booked the talk and hung out afterwards – we had Wisconsin beer in cans and potato chips in little bags, your typical student refreshments – actually formed an escort to walk me to the bus stop. And they waited with me – one even got onto the bus with me – and they all stayed on the sidewalk 'til the bus pulled away. Those kids were great! They were so strong, so into being my bodyguards, my security team.

Why I'm telling this is to say that experience – with their malevolent presence – was crucial education for me. Cops and counter-protestors at anti-war rallies had never made me feel afraid the way those people did. Really. I felt, when I walked out onto the sidewalk, kind of a concentrated hating, and their screaming was strange, crazy and robotic, repeating canned slogans and Bible phrases. Made me think what it was like for Black folks in the civil rights movement, you know? So that was my first time, my first encounter with them. *You* know all about them – you came up in their scene, right? You've had to deal with them from the jump, for years. But that was my first time, and it was early – it was the beginning of their move to terrorism.

Claudia says, Yeah. It was definitely different for the Janes. We knew we had the backing of the majority of the people, the population of the USA thought so differently then. That's why *Roe* could be brought to the Court, and could win in '73. For us, the hardest thing probably was getting all the necessary connections, knowledge and skills – for you, maybe the hardest thing will be getting to use them.

Betsy says, I bet one hard thing will be knowing – by "women's intuition" I suppose – which pregnant woman is a spy, working for the antis. Which one coming through is wearing a wire. It was no romance then; sure as shit it won't be now. Our phones were tapped, like capturing your email, hacking. In fact, it's way more dangerous now; it's a lot less possible to be secret and private, fifty years on.

That's for sure! This ain't no "adventure." With private for-profit prisons and legal torture and the Roberts court? Here in the USA version of Weimar Germany? Sometimes in these past few months I think I'm crazy, literally out of my mind, to be planning this. Keesha groans and puts her head back like she's searching the ceiling for an opening, a ladder going up and out.

It may be we'll do this totally offline, Joanie says. Seriously, we may have to do this off-the-grid – spoken words only, meeting people outside, face-to-face for everything. Deeply old school. Historic! That'll take big work.

Whatever else needs to be considered, the *work* is in the center, Lucy declares. Learning the work. Like this: What we did was, the first thing we learned, first thing the Janes actually *did* when we learned to be abortion medics – we started with longterms, women who were past twelve or thirteen weeks, because (you probably know this) even though longterms are much harder for the women, they're actually much easier to do when it's illegal. Simpler procedures. Because all you're doing is inducing a miscarriage; the women have to go through a painful experience, but the necessary skills for making that happen are easy to learn – and the ways we did it are still good ways. Not as simple as giving medical abortion drugs is now, but simple. If we – I mean *you* – can get the drugs like the Service did, from a friendly neighborhood pharmacist, that'll be fabulous.

Wait, Betsy says. Is there such a thing anymore, Lucy? Aren't drug stores all corporate chains now? I suppose you could hook up with some Rite-Aid or Walgreen pharmacist – might even be easier for them in a huge corporation, hm? We only had the Leuenbach paste for a little while; then we couldn't get it any more and had to do it by hand – is that how it went? Do you remember more, or different, Lu? Claudia?

Wait, Annie says. Before you talk about the paste – you got it from Canada, right? I read about it in that Bard thesis – hey! that's got to be what the guy in the motel used for your mother, Letta) – I have to ask: this word "longterm" – what's it actually mean? *How* long? Is there a cut-off point we should agree on? Like, how far pregnant does a woman have to be when we say, No, we don't do that? And what about this "partial-birth" thing the antis invented? What do *you* think?

Do we even need to agree about that? Gloria says. Can't each Jane have her own opinion, her own line, so that women who want to be done at 24 weeks can get done by somebody who does *that*? Does there have to be a rule about how many weeks a woman can be and still get an abortion? I don't think so. The docs didn't all agree when it was legal; some of them wouldn't do anybody past twelve weeks, and only a couple heroes stepped up to handle late term abs after Dr. Tiller's assassination in 2009. And listen, let's not assume everybody who signs up with us to do this work is already some kind of trained medic; you weren't, were you? None of you came in with medical experience, right?

Hey, Glor. Are you assuming all of us will be doing abortions? I mean, won't some of us just deal with counseling, logistics, connections, reconnaissance, legal work, security, even transportation? I know that was true with the Janes, Jill says, not sure what her own tasks will be – should be, ought to be – when she and her friends become felons.

Right, no – I get that. I'm talking about this particular thing, just this policy decision thing I'm asking about.

And the answer is yes, Gloria, says Betsy. We did do it that way; we did a lot of things that way, like when Denah and Suzanne were both pregnant at the same time and some Janes wanted them to stop doing abortion work when they started to show. We argued, and in some cases – like that one – we made policy for the group but really, individual Janes did what they felt ok about doing – or not.

Annie asks, What did you decide about the two pregnant Janes?

They kept working, Claudia says. Some of us didn't like it, some of us didn't care one way or the other, and some of us thought they were the best example of the service's politics we could ever hope to have.

I'm guessing everybody here knows that great slogan: "Abortion – as early as possible, as late as necessary." We should have that on bumper stickers, embroidered samplers, t-shirts – tattoos, even. Since you ask, I'll say that for *now*, for *this*, I completely agree with Gloria; I don't think you need, or should have, a group policy, Betsy tells them.

Bernie jumps in – Sounds like what we *do* need is training for procedures at each stage of fetal development; how should we deal with that? Some of us already have, or are getting, medical training. And we can probably get a certain amount of information from formerly legal providers, docs, nurse practitioners and midwives who are our friends. Though there's lots of public knowledge now, lots available online, you have to wade through garbage. There's more good stuff from other countries, places where the bad guys aren't in charge of everybody's mind. And there must be more providers who are willing to do it underground now. Right? Right?

There's a pause here, a conversational hold, and then Lucy says, There may still be very few. Bound to be crooks who've jumped in for the money, like that shithead arrested in Pennsylvania in 2011, knowing there're so many desperate women – but good ones? I don't know. It's really true that people in this country didn't use to think about these issues the same ways they do now. It *was* different then. No, seriously; our language was different, our thinking about morality, the concepts we dealt with – all of that. Not only you young ones, even people our age think and talk in different ways now – thanks, she tips her imaginary hat, to the anti-abortion movement and their government and media servants. You have to think about what that means.

Claudia says, Like the idea of abstinence being taken seriously by anybody as a way to keep young women – kids! – from getting pregnant. That is so stupid; we'd have thought it was a joke if somebody offered it for consideration, and yet government's *still* putting dollars into it. It's not like I wouldn't have *wanted* my daughter to abstain from heterosexual intercourse when she was in high school. (Anything but fucking – that's my idea of heaven for girls: sex without fear! Wasn't there a book with that title?) But I never imagined she *would*. Anyway, turns out high school kids who take abstinence pledges, for health or for Jesus or whatever, pretty much break the pledge by 18, if not sooner.

Letta's knitting, and the yarn spills off her lap as she leans in to say, Listen, girls are relieved to escape the pressure – like having to give blow jobs and hand jobs at parties to guys they don't even really know, or assuming every date has to end with fucking. That's got to be part of the appeal: abstinence is a hideout. Then, when they get older, they can handle it. I sure *hope* they can, anyway. If I ever find out my Noah pressured a girl that way, I'd have to hurt him.

How about the abortion-is-murder thing? I never heard *any*body say "abortion is murder" in the '60s or '70s – certainly not before the Hyde amendment, and what was that, '76? That all came with the antis' focus on the fetus – before them, we virtually never talked about fetuses, the way so many people do now, as "babies." Only when women got pregnant on purpose; those, everybody called babies from the get-go. We did talk about how tough it was to get good prenatal care, how it was practically impossible to have a home birth –

Gloria interrupts: That's still true! It's totally insane! Hospitals are terrifying!

– right, that's still the ugly truth. And this was way before high caesarean rates and the absurd percentage of induced births. Oh, stop me, somebody! Don't let me get started on all that! Betsy laughs at herself.

Nobody here will disagree with you, Bets, says Lucy. But you know, a lot of the antis have changed their focus – even with all their success and power, they lost ground about twenty years ago because of so obviously not caring about women's lives. That's when they started getting all mumsy, talking about women-as-mothers, moms&babies, lalala. Not the assassins and the bombers or the religious freaks, but a good chunk of the anti crowd.

We did know there were people against abortion, people who said it was wrong – I always assumed they were brainwashed by religion because I knew a lot of Catholics – maybe I knew something about Mormons, too? Actually, I can't remember if I knew anything about the Latter Day Saints then, probably knew only that Sherlock Holmes story, and later learned more from Tony Kushner – *Angels in America*. Now, of course, their legislation of stupidity and cruelty is burned into my mind, partly thanks to the Romney campaign, I guess. In Utah, they almost trumped the Pope for rigidity and mindlessness in 2010. I guess they couldn't see the success in their future.

Me too, says Claudia. What did I know? I sure didn't know back then that the church had a history of changing policy about abortion – like most people, even my Catholic husband, I thought they'd *always* been against it, and birth control too. I was shocked when I found out they'd had different policies over time, different popes changing the rules and everything, some even liberal – for their own time and place, I mean. Anyway, there was definitely no serious large-scale movement toward fundamentalism among US Protestants, so the Catholic church didn't have that alliance going, the strong connection they have now.

We – the good guys, the home team – are too afraid to talk about the heavy stuff in public, like about killing and morality. That was a strategic error made years ago in the movement, and it still hurts us. It helped them get support for Roverturn, for sure. We should be talking about *everything* – just like the bad guys. They don't *own* motherhood, families, ethics and God, but if we never mention any of that, it sure looks like they do. That's a BIG mistake, Lucy says.

I think about them – the antis. I think how, right now, they must be talking like we're talking. And they have friendships like ours but with their kind of ideas and politics. So they make jokes, or pretend, or try for real honesty and truth just like we do – but all of it inside that fucked-up way they see the world, Jill says.

You really think that, Jill? You think they *struggle* with this? I don't. I think their ignorance allows for tremendous certainty – I mean especially the faith-based ones, the ones who take direction from religious leaders. Letta knits faster, clicking her needles and her tongue.

Oh, who cares? Joanie puts her elbows on the table, hard, and leans in. *I* don't think that. I think they're totally intellectually compromised – at best – morally and ethically narrowed to a *sliver*, and they don't do this kind of talking. But I don't want to spend our time imagining them. Let's put a hold on nice-girl empathy and get back to policy, and practice. Like, one reason we don't talk about that stuff in public, to the media or politicians, is we haven't discussed it enough in private, among ourselves. So we're not clear; we don't have an analysis, a coherent argument – as a movement, I mean. We don't have our shit together on this; lots of *us* are confused and ignorant. Like you were just saying, we've been affected by the propaganda of the religious right; we even use their language. Don't all of you hear perfectly intelligent people – even people working for legal abortion – call the anti-abortion movement the "pro-life" movement, like, every damn day?

She sits back. Our brains have been, oh, not washed, but maybe rinsed? Especially the youngest ones of us – not many of these newly-committed-to-knitting women think and talk like the Queen of Flying Needles over here.

Yes, Lucy says. Yes. I think they've affected – I should say *in*fected – even the people who had good politics from before Hyde. We all live in this country, we're all part of this society, and we can't help but "learn" what they're teaching. You've gotta be waaaay off the grid to escape, no matter how old you are.

So then, what *do* you think? Gloria asks the group. What do *we* think? What do we think about killing fetuses? At any and every stage of development. Setting the bad guys aside, let's talk about what *we* think, let's say how we feel about the heaviest issues – like, is it murder? What *is* murder? What's the difference between *killing* and *murder*? There're so many kinds of killing most people think are ok, what about *that*?

Self-defense for sure, you know, "stand your ground" – and especially like when cops and soldiers do it. The military kills lots of babies, *real* babies, *born* babies, all the time, probably every day. On top of that, for sure we need to get right about the heavy business that goes down in communities of color, in city neighborhoods and on reservations: the notion that abortion is *genocide*, played up bigtime by anti-abortion churches and their allies, funded heavily by the right wing. How to talk about that? We have to be thinking and talking about *all* of this – a whole lot more than we do.

Oh yeah – that gets a certain amount of play in my family, Annie says. Mostly from one uncle who likes to bait me because he already knows what I think. But I could use some attention to that, yeah.

Gloria takes a breath and says, We heard the original Janes were all white women, pretty much middle class, all straight – and married too. Is that true? And if it is, what differences do we think will come from our differences? Could an all-white model be useful, even?

Whoa, I never thought about that, says Jill. You think maybe it'd be hard to do this work as one group, together? Maybe we could have separate groups, operating separately but sharing information when necessary? Then we wouldn't have to worry about our differences getting in the way.

Ah, yes: Separate but equal – an interesting model. I think that's been tried, Jill; it didn't work out, says Annie.

True enough, says Claudia. We started out all white. We were mostly middle class in the early days, though not completely, even then. And in open conversation, in talking at meetings, it was like we assumed, if we even *thought* about it, that everybody was straight; some of us were either clueless or closeted. But by the time the Service shut down, a few months after the *Roe* decision, there was at least one Black woman in the group – and there was a Black law student who helped out sometimes; a Latina joined in the last year too. We'd always been diversified by class, and we definitely were *not* all married. Some never had been and some of those who were to start with weren't by the time it was over. I'm what you all would probably call old-school in this regard, but Betsy and Lucy have stellar credentials.

Bernie says, Women's Studies classes must've really helped, right?

Lucy takes an audible breath and says, First of all, sweetheart, not everybody goes to college – like me, for instance; so let's keep that in mind. And second (she pauses dramatically) – wait, no. Not second. No. *Most of all:* I *am* Women's Studies: *I'm* your goddamn homework. You think we didn't know from our own lives what *you* read about in books? Our actual lives are what you were taught to call "feminist theory." Abortion work is what we did, but it's not *all* we did. We lived the lives that got put in those books. And the Janes were the ones who, no matter what else was going on, secretly committed multiple felonies every goddamn week for more than four years because we always knew this whole thing was about us, about *women*, about *women's liberation*.

This speech is followed by silence.

Keesha and Joanie lock eyes and Keesha says, Let's stop to take a deep breath – six deep breaths. Let's move into the living room, get away from this table. And let's think about Bernice Johnson Reagon, what she said about coalition, about making alliances across difficult differences. You know: if it's easy, if it feels good – it's not working.

Joanie sighs dramatically. I guess this is working, then – right? How about we just keep talking about abortion: what it is, what it means, where it fits into *all* women's struggles; let's just do that together.

There's quiet in the group. Then Lucy says, What the hell, why not? I can probably do that. Problem is, I care about this too much. But you picked me up at the airport and you gave me supper; I am a gracious guest, however touchy. Bernie, let me get you some tea.

The women get up, clear the table and move to the living room couch, rocking chair and floor pillows.

In the kitchen, choosing among herbals, fruit flavors, organic greens, Indian dark and a big jar of dried ginger root, Betsy says to Lucy, What do you really think of these young ones, Lu?

What do I think? I think they're cute. All that passion, those bright eyes and good minds? They're just what they should be, just what they need to be in this hard time. That's what I think, and besides, like any Jane knows – you don't have to approve or love each other to do this work. You probably remember there were Janes who didn't think my schtick was funny, didn't appreciate my recitations of "The Curette Chronicles" – so who am I to diss these kids?

When everybody's settled in, tea mugs in hand, honey and lemon on a low table, Gloria says, We're gonna need a series of discussion groups – along with or even before we get into the action.

We've got to have talking points, we've got to at least pick out, and work on, the issues media and politicians are always gonna ask about. And we need to get solid, get comfortable, in our own work – even if we don't all agree, we need to have conversations like this. And we don't want to be standing in front of a camera with our mouths open and no words coming out if somebody asks us for a soundbite. For every

YouTuber with a cameraphone, we need to get it right, Keesha says.

Jeez, if we're underground, that won't happen! But even aside from media, you're right about all of us needing this – the whole reproductive justice movement, all the women's health and sexuality people, our local Coalition for sure, says Jill. There has to be a whole lot more thinking and talking together – like *you* did, in rap groups, women's groups, all kinds of work groups.

Don't lose sight of the fact there may be less sympathy now for illegal action, for underground work. Less than there was for *us*, I mean. You've got the ignorance factor, the antis' power. In a way, you're *lucky* the turkeys overturned *Roe*, Betsy says. Because, weak and meaningless as it was by then, it still kept lotsa people off your team. They said, Hey, what's the problem? Abortion's legal. They can't say *that* anymore.

Keesha and Joanie nod.

And you're unlikely to have the kind of underground approval we got from lots of cops, for instance. But look, we can talk about this stuff – I mean, ok, we *should* talk about this stuff – but in our spare time, you know? Like if it's necessary for a policy decision. The main thing is, we – I mean *you* – set up a Service, a network, and you keep it going. That was one of the best things about the old Service: we almost never agreed, all of us, about *any*thing – except that women should be able to get abortions when we need them – everything else was extra, right?

Yes, that's true, Lucy, and it was a strong point – but it could be a weakness now that people have a more negative mindset. This is definitely a "things are different now" issue. And new science – don't forget that part, says Claudia. Women see ultrasound images of fetuses and are encouraged to think of them as *baby pictures*, so if they don't want that "baby," they're made to think of themselves as selfish and cold, cruel if not vicious – if not "murderers." And now the medical industry is able to keep fetuses alive from earlier points in gestation; they've got more sophisticated equipment, viability's defined so differently – all of that is part of the situation. Instead of simply being useful science for wanted babies, it's all been put to work for the anti-abortion argument.

I've always resented (actually, I've been afraid of) those science guys, all so hot to make people in petri dishes and test tubes – creepy Frankensteins that they are. With their uterus envy, their caesareans and scary drugs, their insistence that women give birth in hospitals on our backs – don't you think all that goes with the man-on-top position in hetero sex? I think it's about being able to get rid of women altogether – to have a world where they can have everything they want *without us* and never have to feel bad about the fact that, basically, their only purpose in the species is to deliver sperm. Women make people inside our bodies, feed them from our bodies and nurture their growth for years. They – men – they're like male bees, and they know it. That's gotta be at least part of the reason they're so hostile and violent. Think about it. Think about *them* – some of them even *fuck big plastic dolls*. And soon they'll have robots and droids that're way more "lifelike."

Jill goes on, Lately I've actually thought, oh, they own the whole world anyway. It's been theirs to ruin and they have. The end's much closer than we imagined, so why not just let them have it, you know, go live in the woods until it's over?

What?! Are you crazy? yells Betsy. First of all, I can't believe you think that shit but second of all, if you're right – could she possibly be *right?* – I wanna fight them for it. I'm sixty-five years old but I'll strap on body armor. Why should we let them have the world? Why should we give up and let them have it?

All right, you guys. All right. As long as we're doing Biology, Philosophy and Psych 101 – and maybe Science Fiction or Fantasy Lit? – I've got a question. I'm serious when I ask this, don't think I'm not – I mean, I'm a medical student, and I'm straight, and I'm 26 years old, and I've had classes with the most poisonously anti-abortion prof at OHSU and I've got a grandmother who's a far right Christian – she freaked when I did clinic defense in high school – but I have never been able to figure out where all this *comes* from. Bernie stands up and keeps talking. I mean, why *do* they think the way they do? Why *did* the US anti-abortion movement happen? What's *really* bothering them? I've studied this history, so I know that nobody else, *in any other country, at any other time, ever* created a homegrown anti-abortion movement on anything *like* this scale. And we know all their "pro-life" talk is fake – that's not what they're about. Their movement's not against the death penalty, they're not against war or police shoot-to-kill, they don't say a word about torture, they don't care much about poverty, they haven't set up a system to take care of abandoned kids – she stops to take big breath here – and lots of them don't like contraception either, so they don't seem to want women to be able to *prevent* unplanned pregnancy. They don't even seem to be working to clean up the planet; they're not stopping *that* kind of destruction-of-life. So, what is it, *really*, that makes them hate abortion so much? I'm serious – what *is* it? This drives me crazy, and besides, I have to know what to tell my daughter.

- *They hate women, and abortion's all about women.*
- *Oh, don't be silly – lots of them* are *women.*
- *So what – haven't you ever heard of internalized oppression?*
- *They don't hate women consciously, they've just learned – from really old ideas sometimes, maybe most of the time – to*

devalue and despise women, including themselves if they are women.

• I think she's right – I think women, and especially female sexuality, are still damned, blamed, considered disgusting. I mean, why is fellatio ok but cunnilingus yucky? A penis in the mouth is super-cool? They don't even wipe it off after they pee.

Keesha says, Let's shorten Bernie's question to, Why should anybody have such intense negative feelings against abortion as to create and foster a giant political movement that even includes terrorism and assassination? And if we go with the sexuality thing, it comes to this: Why do so many people still distrust, dislike and think so little of women? How come that's still happening? The Super Bowl? Hollywood's sexist movie-makers? Thing is, female sexuality is feared (or envied: multiple orgasms!) most especially when power's involved. Individual exceptions aside, women are still not supposed to have the power to make life & death choices. Look what happens to women serving in the military, armed and trained as they are – rape stats off the charts! Folks here don't have thousands of years of images of Kali to help them understand the complexity; the euphemism "right to choose" got used instead of just talking about the right to abortion because the idea of women being that powerful, having the power to create and cut off life – is way too scary.

Lucy says, Well, female power is all wrapped up with sexuality. Not only in the oldest ways, like with Kali, Lilith, Eve, Mary and on through patriarchal history to Islam. Abortion, let's face it, is all about women and sex. Pregnancy is evidence of sex – unless you turn it into maternity by keeping the baby and, you know, defusing the whole situation.

Claudia says, Oh, just read Right-Wing Women by Andrea Dworkin – it's all in there; then we don't have to go on about this.

- *Can we get back on track here?*
- *This* is *our track.*
- *I can't believe we're doing this. We only have a few days to talk with these women!*
- *Let's discuss things even some antis are willing to see as reasons, justifications for abortion – the exceptions.*
- *Hey, good name for a band! The Exceptions.*

Annie says, I think it's important for us to know what we think and how we feel about the reasons; I mean the *ordinary* stuff. Everybody talks all the time about the big three – rape, incest, life-of-the-mother. But we all know most abortions, the *huge* majority, are not about that. And everybody's reluctant to talk about that because – because, because what? Is it that ordinary stuff is boring?

No, no, no; it's because the ordinary stuff's not "sympathetic." It doesn't make women into miserable victims. Even in Canada and England, where they seem to have pretty good laws, women have had to give "acceptable" reasons, claim to be sick or depressed or whatever. Their decisions are medicalized; they have to have their rationales – their excuses, like getting out of class – ok'd by a doctor or two doctors or some panel of social workers. They can't just say: *I've decided not to carry this pregnancy to term. This was a mistake, an error. User error. I don't want to have this baby. This baby would not have a good life.* The ordinary stuff, the everyday facts of life, about women being forced to have children they don't want – *and* facts about the lives of those children – that stuff makes everybody see, makes everybody have to admit: ordinary heterosexual activity, the kind lots of people do for fun, *risks pregnancy.* You do it to have a good time but – uh oh! – you make a person. User error's ok for software, but not for people. How too ironic, says Gloria. Nobody's immune to this kind of thinking, either. Sometimes I worry if my kids can tell I made Miranda on purpose and Eladio before I got myself together.

Annie says, Right. As if *people* didn't make software. Look, we know that lots of women and girls get pregnant by mistake just because they're human – it's literally an accident – we're all fallible, the birth control we use is fallible (I even know a guy whose vasectomy healed, and he started shooting sperm again) and relationships we have with men are totally fallible!

So many women are ignorant, or too young to handle the emotional situation. There's often intense pressure from a boy or man. That hasn't changed – only the vocabulary and costumes are different, says Claudia.

Right, yes, that's a big part of what I mean, Annie says. That sure is what happened to me. That's probably why I'm sitting in this room right now – well, in the realm of cause and effect.

What do you mean? Betsy asks.

Here's a short version of my own fallibility story: I'm one of the ones who went – right out of high school – into the army. I know what Keesha was talking about, about the military. I went for the college money. You know. I was a smart kid, but I was still a *kid*. Not only did I go for the line the recruiter gave me, once I was in I went for some other lines too. Talk about "intense pressure" from boys and men! It's like I was a tree and they were loggers.

Hey, Annie-Jeff, don't be so hard on yourself. You were eighteen years old and far from home, Letta says.

What happened? Lucy asks.

Typical. Classic. You could probably tell the story yourself. I was flattered by so much attention, I fucked a few guys carelessly – and by "carelessly" I mean "without taking care." So, surprise, surprise, I got pregnant. The really *big* surprise, though, was that my "full benefits" healthcare plan, as a soldier in the US Army, did not cover abortion. I mean, I could've been in the Peace Corps, I could've been working at the Post Office, any Federal government job – you know this, but I didn't – in all of those, they don't pay. Thank you, Henry Hyde. I was stunned. I did have the silver lining effect, though – I had a leave coming, and I went home. I'll skip the family impact scenes – we can close the door on those. Here in Portland, at eleven weeks, I got a vacuum D&C from a really cool doc. But, anyway, I was so fried, so pissed off about my federal government not-really-insurance-after-all that I didn't re-up when my time came. I'd also found out the college money didn't work like the guy at my high school recruitment fair said it would – or not *said*, but let us all think – you know, however they're, like, trained to do it. So I became a civilian (and now it looks like I'm about to become a criminal). But my point – my point in telling this embarrassing story – is that "accidents" are *so* often about being normal, just normal fallible people. The user error thing.

Bernie says, Later, maybe, I'll tell *my* abortion story. No – not now, not here. I prefer to get drunk to tell it.

You?! Drunk?! I'll stay up late for that, Keesha says. Then I'll tell mine. You careful and lucky types with no personal abortion experience, you'll just have to put up with it, and be our designated drivers.

While you people are into admitting your own mistakes, let's not forget contraceptive failure, Joanie says. Our pharma friends and their statistics! In fact, let's not forget contraceptive *danger*! Synthetic hormones, implants under our skin or inside our uteruses, pills with generic chemical compositions for a definitely NOT generic population – *all that*.

I'd like us to talk about what it means to be forced to make and raise a person, and what that means for the life of a person who gets made and raised like that, says Keesha.

Yes! Like Annie said, there's an *accident*: Children suffer because of a momentary lapse, because something blind-sided you, maybe something you couldn't possibly control. Claudia's voice rises. Something went wrong. Somebody runs in front of your car, runs out of an alley as you happen to be driving by. Or your car malfunctions – the wipers stop working in a rainstorm and you can't see, or your brakes go out, or you glance at the clock in the same second somebody changes lanes right in front of you without signaling. That's why it's *an accident*. (I'm not including cell phone morons here.) Getting pregnant while conscientiously using a diaphragm when you – actually, *I* – have two little kids already, that's *an accident*.

Enough with the car, Lucy says. How does the "accident" thing translate into getting pregnant? Why *isn't* the phrase "human error" used more often by the good guys, by us? Is it because that'd be yet another opportunity for blaming women?

I want to talk about why people keep on making so many people! Isn't it really just because the science guys are into this exciting lab experiment they get funded for? Then drug companies figure out how to make a ton of money from convincing women to use the new thing – or convincing doctors to convince women to use stuff that's literally experimental! You may think I'm just into my Frankenstein rant here, but I know we have to deal with this, says Jill.

Do they not think ahead, think of what it will be, *who* it will be, how it will be for that kid in the world once it's born? The goddamn motherhood imperative, yells Gloria. Compulsory motherhood, like Adrienne Rich wrote before I was born! Different reasons now: Mothers don't "work for the army" anymore, women aren't pushed into motherhood to create the people needed to grow food – that was sooooo long ago, so two centuries ago. Not even the "workforce," sad shrunken thing *that* is. Now it's all about making consumers. Have children – so you can accessorize them.

Calm down. Who are you – Emma Goldman? Besides, we can only cover so much, we've got only a few hours left. Letta's needles click when she talks.

Lucy says, You're all making me think of women I've known. My friend Bonnie, whose condom broke when her husband was suicidally depressed, and my cousin Reva – she was addicted to painkillers when her IUD failed. My own mother, who already had five kids when she got pregnant the same week my dad got called back up by the Navy. But listen – let's get back to planning mode. We - *you* - ought to look at the way Irish women used to go to England for their abortions – to help figure out how to do it here, now. Or Dr. Gomperts' boat! Could we – could *you* – float a small clinic on the Columbia? Or just outside the two state lines, where the river flows into the Pacific? And remember, for the earliest ones, that doc and her team are on the web now too.

Gloria says, I always say we need more time, more meetings.

Annie laughs, suddenly and loud. Yeah? And do you always say where that time, for those meetings, is gonna come from? I mean, like in real life? – your real life, and mine?

Gloria says, It's always a hassle, isn't it? And talking to these ladies makes it obvious – it always has been! So I guess it always will be. But somehow – and I admit I don't really understand how this happens – a whole lot of work actually gets done.

Bernie smiles. Yeah! Are we cool, or what?

We are definitely cool, Keesha says. Definitely.

Monumental

By Stephanie Daley

Construction has begun on the mall for our newest national monument. The award-winning design, chosen from more than three hundred original entries, took top honors among the finalists. All entries were offered anonymously to a prestigious panel of judges. The announcement of the winner caused a rush of surprise – and some consternation – when organizers and developers discovered their top design was created by a team of high school seniors from Waukegan, Illinois. But the design itself, the judges insist, is what matters.

The monument design team members' parents are very proud of Jamayah Hurston, Tina Valerio, Lily Wong and Natalie Berger. The girls, all students in the Art & Industry track at Waukegan's Lakeside Technical High School, had kept their contest entry a secret. "We never thought we'd win, and we didn't want to be, like, embarrassed, so we didn't tell anybody. We didn't want anybody saying we were losers, you know, a bunch of extincts," said Ms. Wong. Their teacher, Josie Winfrey, is very proud: "I knew they spent lots of extra time in the shop, hanging around after school. I never guessed something like this was on their minds! I've never assigned anything like this either. They told me they spotted the competition notice while using the shop computer – I guess that justifies the online zine subscription to our principal!" Ms. Winfrey hopes that all four of her students will go on to college. Smiling, she says they have – now – what she calls "a darn good shot at some scholarships."

The team members say they were inspired by what they learned about the VietNam Memorial, designed decades ago by prestigious monument architect Maya Lin when she too was quite young, chosen by judges who did not know her identity. But these young women are not simply copying that earlier winner, a monument many commentators call the most visited and most revered public memorial in the United States. The team did decide, early in their work, that Ms. Lin was right to use the names of the men – "and boys" they insist, "lots of the ones who died were really boys, some from our school," said Tina Valerio when questioned by a reporter. "Yeah, we all know that, everybody totally knows that, and we wanted to be sure our design, like, shows the truth," added Ms. Berger at a group interview. "I don't think our work reminded the judges of Maya Lin's design just because we used names. Lots of memorials have lists of names, even in cemeteries, like when lots of people die from the same thing," said Ms. Hurston.

Unlike Ms. Lin's sharply geometric wall of gleaming black, the new memorial is what some are calling an abstraction, a rounded shape with many curving indentations. The final piece will be three stories high and will cover the space of a city block; the model for the structure resembles a giant rock, agate red, irregularly surfaced and highly polished. The names of women and girls will be cut into the stone at random – no lists or lines, no alphabetical or chronological order. Each one, Ms. Hurston says, "is an ordinary name in the USA. Like, anybody's name? We did that because we want them to stand for *more* names, we want people to think about their own names when they see these. We did it because lots of women, especially girls around our age – no, especially *younger* girls – hardly ever get their names put down anywhere important besides their birth certificate. Unless they play sports. For those girls it's different. We know that."

Packets sent to the media include full color drawings of the winning model, blueprints of the site layout, and 39 names, called by the four young designers "the names of responsible mothers who did what had to be done" (*see sidebar*).

Betty Lou Green	Karen Simms	Hannah Ickes
Frankie Papandreou	Alice Beecham	Ayeesha Daniels
Ellen Aldredge	Layla Ng	Deanna Smithers
Anna Sanchez	Ronna Chang	Mary Frances Ryan
Mary Catherine Stanley	Maryana Podolska	Rosamaria Santiago
Julie Rosenberg	Carrie Steinhaupt	Penny Jones
Jane Brigham Smith	Fannie Rae Toller	Kyoko Takahashi
Vera Miniver	Sadie Nussbaum	Una Petain
Paula Yazzie	Amina Sagal	Lucinda Yoder
Ona Haddad	Sarah Rezkolnyi	Angela Roncalli
LaTonya Veatch	Louise Kincaid	Zora Ortega
Meena Chakravorty	Yvonne Blackwing	Lisa Farrell
Nora Zambjorska	Terrelle Washington	Sandra Brown

At selected sites around the central monument will be booths that run videos of typical stories – dramatizations in which some of the most renowned performers of our time will play the parts of those "responsible mothers who did what had to be done." The design team will not disclose the names of the actors on their wish list for these short movies, but all say they are hoping to cast some of their favorites. Team members are providing screenwriters with story ideas, drawn from the lives of their own families and friends – for whom, they quickly tell interviewers, they have "made up fake names." They've even offered titles – *Hyde and Seek* is the first one on their list.

Ms. Wong says, "Everybody knows stories like these, but seeing them acted out, like in a movie or on tv, even a retro-reality show or YouTube, makes you think about it different ways, you know? That always makes something amazing happen in your head, in your mind, while you watch. Like, these people I babysat for had a story. The woman – I'm calling her Geeta – had one abortion and two children. Geeta was only married three months when she had the abortion, and then she had the two kids three years and five years later, and they planned those two so it'd be just right."

Ms. Hurston tells about a woman she named Shanna, who had four abortions and four children from two husbands. "Shanna actually never wanted to be a mother but everybody expected her to do it. Two kids was enough for her first husband, so she had two abortions when she got pregnant by accident. But then her second husband wanted his own children, so she did it all over again – and it was two and two the second time!"

Ms. Berger tells about a woman she calls Abby, who had three abortions and one child. "Abby says she had one just to show she could do it – she didn't like to think there was anything she couldn't do, but she hated getting fat."

Ms. Valerio hopes to get her favorite telenovela star to play the lead in the story of Margo, who had one boyfriend, three children and no abortions. "She was nineteen and they were moving in together, so when they did it she thought it wouldn't matter, but the babies were always wanting something, always making noise, always making a mess. And *she* still wanted to go out and play, you know?"

Visitors to the monument will be able to walk along the smooth curves of the surface, where they'll encounter the names engraved there. It is the intention and hope of the design team that visitors will also sit down on the grass or one of the many benches included in the model, and read the plaques that tell how it happened:

The condom broke.   The IUD failed.   The diaphragm slipped.   The implant made me sick.   One time we got foolish and this is what came from it.   He wouldn't wear it.   He wouldn't wait for me to put it in.   We got a little drunk and went for a long walk on the beach and then, well, you know.   He threw away my pills.   He didn't pull out in time.   They pushed me down on the floor in the basement.   The priest said we should use the calendar. The doctor said it was an experiment.   We were in love.

In one unusual aspect of the plan, high above the grass and benches will be carved words that no one who visits the monument can see. The team has daringly stretched their audience by including what cannot be seen by visitors, and their rationale seemed sound to the judges. Danforth Humphrey, Dean Emeritus of the Capitol School of Architecture and Design, and Charles Cadbury, former art critic for the Los Angeles Times, explained what they and their fellow judges find praiseworthy in this unconventional design element. "The carvings scattered around the monument far above ground level are all quotations from writers who addressed these issues before our youthful contest winners ever thought about them – in several cases, before these young women were even born. The carvings, like the names and aphorisms cut around the crowning frieze of so many of our great libraries, represent the philosophical history, if you will, of the present work," said Dean Humphrey. "They are the relevant classics."

(Interviewed by this reporter, the team agreed with that estimate and added, "It's like having a tattoo where nobody sees it when you're all dressed. You won't show it to, like, just anybody, but you always know it's there, and it's really important – to you.")

Though the media packet did not include examples, Mr. Cadbury cited a few: "They've chosen the first line of Gwendolyn Brooks' classic poem, 'The Mother,' which many of us read in school: 'Abortions will not let you forget.' They're using repeated placements of lines from songs as well. There's a veritable manifesto by Tupac (the most notable line in 'Keep Ya Head Up' – a bit shocking in its own time) and selections from the brilliant piece by Digable Planets, 'La Femme Fatale/Fetal' in addition to the refrain from Malvina Reynolds' remarkable song – the part that begins, 'Are you pregnant again, Rosie Jane?' They've gotten permission to use 'How could she keep the baby? She can barely keep her head' from Melissa Etheridge's *All-American Girl*, and there's an extraordinary couplet, if I may call it that, by poet Marilyn Nelson: 'It's not so simple to give a child birth/you also have to give it death.' There are, of course, many more, but I don't want to run on," said the critic.

Despite double-barreled criticism – from longtime foes of abortion and prominent art critics who insist that the monument's use of quoted material and how-it-happened plaques is "didactic," and undercuts "the necessary structural aesthetics" – Ms. Wong, Ms. Hurston, Ms. Berger and Ms. Valerio say they don't think about their critics. They say they have more important things to think about now.

Asked what made them decide to enter the competition, three of the four young winners immediately pointed to Lily Wong. "She started it, for sure," said Ms. Valerio. "Yeah, she dragged us all to this rally at the start of junior year," Ms. Berger said, "where all these women were making speeches. It was sorta like on YouTube from that Occupy Movement back in 2011 – like *that*." "And the thing that really got us," said Ms. Hurston, "I mean all of us, was that the women up there could have been our mothers. I mean, nothing bad on our mothers, but these women were totally ordinary. Not like they were extincts – just *ordinary*, you know?"

Lily Wong herself picked up the chorus. "It was that woman I named Geeta who told me to go, and I was sort of interested but like I didn't want to go alone? So I took my girls. And it turned out to be totally amazing. Seriously. See, these women making speeches were dressed like they ran out of the house to buy some toothpaste or something, totally not famous or important looking, and not super-fancy-smart either. But here's the thing: they were making speeches, walking up there, talking in the microphone – some weren't even as good at it as kids running for student council. But they said such cool things. That was what got us. They said totally cool things. Or maybe it just, like, seemed cool because of who they were, how they looked – I don't know.

Ms. Valerio continued: "Yeah, they said stuff like, 'We did not pretend that we were crazy. We did not get depressed. We did not have regrets. We did not plead insanity – even the temporary kind.' Remember that one? She made everybody laugh! And near the end, right when we were leaving, one of them said, 'We accept responsibility for our actions. We are responsible mothers who have seen many monuments to death and love, but not a one, never a one, that honors us.' That was what she said, wasn't it? Right? That totally knocked us out. I mean, like, that just knocked us out, because we're – we *used to be*! – just sooooo used to never getting credit, you know? For anything? That was it. That started us thinking, so when Natalie found the contest, we were all over it. Know what I mean? We were just all over it."

contact: stepdaley@ding.chgo

Another Note to Readers

While I was writing about abortion, I was also writing about tattooing. I'm almost always working on at least two projects and they often cross-pollinate, sort of move into each other. When that started happening with these, I realized I'd gotten my first tattoo just a few weeks after the Roe decision in 1973. Then I started to put the two together on purpose. First I thought about how both are related to body consciousness, decisions about our physical lives, having control over our own bodies. Then I considered the special technology/ equipment required for both to be done skillfully in good health – though simple methods have been used all over the globe for thousands of years in both cases. Both include decisions affecting people's lives in long-lasting ways.

Pretty soon, I saw that access-to and appreciation-of tattooing has grown – amazingly – at the same time access-to and appreciation-of abortion has declined. One has been a deliberate movement to change people's thinking, driven by huge amounts of money from anti-abortion sources; the other appears to be an organic cross-cultural development. I mean, as far as we know, the right wing has not been funding the rise of tattooing (they're too busy working against sex education, contraception, abortion healthcare and the integrity of women). Here's something I found when I started paying attention: Tattooing has been legal in all 50 states only since 2006 – and, get this – the last state to make it legal was Oklahoma, which four years later passed a law requiring women seeking abortions to first have an ultrasound and listen to a detailed description of the fetus. I've known for a long time that everything is connected, but still – I found some pretty startling things.

Acknowledgements & Gratitude

"Answering the Question" and "Knocking" were first published in *Serving House Journal* in late fall of 2012. An earlier version of "Keesha and Joanie and JANE" was published as a zine by Eberhardt Press in 2013. An earlier version of the story Letta tells about her mother in "Keesha and Joanie and JANE" was part of a piece published in *Feminist Studies* in 2008. An earlier version of "Betsy Is Interviewed for *Tattoo Queen*'s Website Biography Series" appeared with a different title in *Persimmon Tree* in 2007. "Hello. This is Jane." was published in *THE HUMAN* in 2015. "Soon To Be A Major Motion Picture" was published as a prize-winning chapbook by Minerva Rising, appearing in early 2015. "Denah & the Strawberry, Talking" was published in *The Literary Nest* in 2016. A slightly edited version of "Monumental" appeared in the zine *Chasing the Night* #3, in fall of 2016, and another version of "Men of God" appeared in *Chasing the Night* #4, at the end of 2017.

I'm grateful to Daniel Arcana, Peaches Bass, Sarah Boehm, Andrea Carlisle, Cindy Cooper, Jodi Darby, Megan Felling, Jan Johnson, Gwyn Kirk, Stephanie Poggi, BT Shaw, Kate Weck and Erin Yanke for critical reading and serious talking. And I thank Bebe Anderson, Estelle Carol, Lisa Hamilton, Rosie Much, Charles Overbeck, Grace Paley, Gerry Pearson and Bob Simpson for sparks along the way, and David Shields for permission to quote his linked fiction riff. I seriously appreciate some crucial talking by Christine Vachon (who doesn't even know me) when she was onstage at Whitsell Auditorium in Portland, Oregon in the summer of 2011. Jonathan Arlook has been encouraging my writing since 1975 (he prefers the poetry, but as a longtime member of the JANE Men's Auxiliary, he cheers for this book too).

I'm grateful to the Mesa Refuge, the Wurlitzer Foundation, Soapstone, Milepost5 and the Institute for Anarchist Studies – all of which gave me time, space or money in the years these stories were being written.

I'm grateful to the tattoo artists, some of them no longer alive, whose work has been important to me since 1973: Cliff Raven and Buddy McFall in Chicago, Lyle Tuttle in San Francisco, Mary Jane Haake and Don Deaton in Portland, Oregon.

I'm grateful to Ryan Forsythe, the publisher/editor/designer of this book, for his enthusiasm, commitment, and skillful work.

I'm grateful for JANE – the work and the spirit, then and now.

About the Author

Judith Arcana is a Jane, a member of Chicago's pre-Roe underground abortion service. She writes poems, stories, essays and books, including a much-loved biography of Grace Paley (*Grace Paley's Life Stories*) and several poetry collections: *What if your mother, 4th Period English, The Parachute Jump Effect, Announcements from the Planetarium,* and *Here From Somewhere Else,* which received the Editor's Choice Chapbook Award from *Turtle Island Quarterly.* She hosts a poetry show on KBOO in Oregon and online. Born and raised in the Great Lakes region, Judith has lived in the Pacific Northwest since 1995. For more about, and examples of, her work, visit JudithArcana.com.